storyteller

ALSO BY
PATRICIA REILLY GIFF

FOR MIDDLE-GRADE READERS

Wild Girl
Eleven
Water Street
Willow Run
A House of Tailors
Maggie's Door
Pictures of Hollis Woods
All the Way Home
Nory Ryan's Song
Lily's Crossing
The Gift of the Pirate Queen
The Casey, Tracy & Company books

FOR YOUNGER READERS

The Zigzag Kids books
The Kids of the Polk Street School books
The Friends and Amigos books
The Polka Dot Private Eye books

PATRICIA REILLY GIFF

storyteller

WENDY
LAMB
BOOKS

Copyright © 2010 by Patricia Reilly Giff
Map copyright © 2010 by Rick Britton

All rights reserved. Published in the United States by
Wendy Lamb Books, an imprint of Random House Children's Books,
a division of Random House, Inc., New York.

Wendy Lamb Books and the colophon are trademarks of Random House, Inc.

Visit us on the Web! www.randomhouse.com/kids

Educators and librarians, for a variety of teaching tools, visit us at
www.randomhouse.com/teachers

Library of Congress Cataloging-in-Publication Data
Giff, Patricia Reilly.
Storyteller / Patricia Reilly Giff. — 1st ed.
p. cm.
Summary: Forced to spend months at an aunt's house, Elizabeth feels a connection to her ancestor Zee, whose picture hangs on the wall, and who reveals her story of hardships during the Revolutionary War as Elizabeth comes to terms with her own troubles.
ISBN 978-0-375-83888-0 (hc) — ISBN 978-0-375-93888-7 (lib. bdg.) —
ISBN 978-0-375-89744-3 (ebook) [1. Family—Fiction. 2. Fathers and daughters—Fiction. 3. United States—History—Revolution, 1775–1783—Fiction. 4. New York (State)—History—Revolution, 1775–1783—Fiction. 5. Aunts—Fiction.] I. Title.
PZ7.G3626Ss 2010
[Fic]—dc22
2009048130

The text of this book is set in 12-point Goudy.

Book design by Kenny Holcomb

Printed in the United States of America

10 9 8 7 6 5 4 3 2 1

First Edition

Random House Children's Books supports the
First Amendment and celebrates the right to read.

2240

WITH LOVE TO WILLIAM REILLY GIFF,
MY SON BILL,
FOR MORE REASONS THAN I CAN COUNT

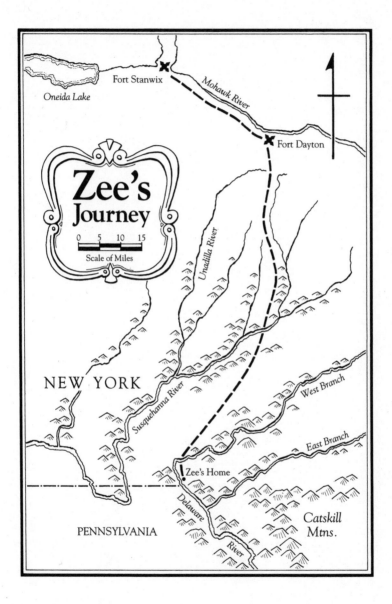

Fort Stanwix

Oneida Lake

Mohawk River

Fort Dayton

N

Zee's
Journey

0   5   10   15
Scale of Miles

Unadilla River

NEW YORK

Susquehanna River

West Branch

East Branch

Zee's Home

Delaware

PENNSYLVANIA

River

Catskill
Mtns.

TWENTY-FIRST CENTURY

School's over; the weekend's here. Elizabeth heads for home. She'll put her feet up on the bench in the kitchen, read her library book, and finish off the brownies she and Pop made last night.

What could be better?

She trudges around to the back door, passing the living room, then Pop's workroom. She can see him through the window. He's long and lanky, his hair a little gray around the temples. He's leaning over his table, working on one of his carvings. On a shelf above his head, wooden animals march along in a row, and a face mask glares out at her. Weird. She tilts her head, picturing someone wearing that mask; a girl maybe, trying to look fierce. Her name would be . . .

Pop spots her. "Elizabeth?"

She climbs the steps, pushes open the door, and drops her backpack inside. "Hey, Pop," she calls.

"What were you doing out there?" he asks, coming into the kitchen.

"Just . . ." Embarrassed, she doesn't know what to say. "Just nothing, I guess."

She sees now that he has a line between his eyebrows.

Trouble. She tries to think about what she's done, or what she hasn't done. She grins to herself. Maybe it's something he hasn't done. The breakfast dishes are still in the sink; a plate with sandwich crusts is on the table.

"How about a hot chocolate to warm you up?" he says, taking the milk out of the refrigerator.

Still that frown. What's coming? She reaches into the cabinet for a couple of crackers.

"Listen, Elizabeth," he says. "I have to go to Australia. I've been asked to show my carvings at a university in Melbourne."

Australia! A million miles away. She blows air through her mouth. It means staying with Mrs. Eldridge and her fat bulldog with his horrible breath. But she can do that. She's done it dozens of times before when he's been away teaching or selling his carvings.

Pop runs a hand through his graying hair. "I called your aunt Libby. She says you can stay with her." He reaches for the box of cocoa. "She's only two or three hours away."

Elizabeth stares at him, a saltine halfway to her mouth. Her mother's sister? Elizabeth has seen her maybe twice in her life. Libby, a scientist, who probably spends her days in a dusty laboratory, working with little dishes of who knows what. She sends odd Christmas and birthday cards, her writing so small you can hardly make it out, and she doesn't have kids. Of course she doesn't.

"Libby!" Elizabeth explodes. "I don't even know what she looks like. I'll stay with Mrs. Eldridge."

Pop turns away to stir the milk on the stove. "Mrs. Eldridge is moving away."

"Alexa, then—she's my best friend, after all."

He pours the milk into a glass. It's so hot the glass cracks. Elizabeth watches the milk sizzle out across the stove, and thinks about her mother, who died in a car accident so long ago she can't even remember her.

Pop stands in front of her. "I might be gone several weeks, Elizabeth. It can't be helped. I wish it could. I don't want to go without you. I don't want to leave you for so long."

He hesitates, a dishcloth in his hands. "But it's time for you to know your mother's family. I've been feeling that for a while. Libby spent a lot of the last few years doing research in Canada, otherwise I'd have asked her sooner."

Elizabeth doesn't answer. She goes inside to turn on the television, pressing up the volume until everything around her vibrates.

Pop comes to the door. "I'm sorry, Elizabeth. I'm so sorry. This will be important to us, really. It'll mean more money, commissions for more carvings."

She turns away from him. Libby. A different school. She'll miss chorus and gymnastics. He's not worried about her missing school. One time she missed a few weeks. "You'll catch up," he'd said, knowing she would.

It's so unfair, but she knows there's no hope of changing

his mind. Not by banging her bedroom door shut all week, not by skipping breakfast, not by saying she's sick and can't go to school.

~

The next Friday Pop brings two duffel bags from the basement. She stuffs almost everything she owns into them while he straightens the house and locks everything up.

They drive through a spring snow. It coats the windows like feathers; the windshield wipers drum back and forth.

"If this works out, I'll go back to Australia next year," Pop says. "Maybe you can go with me someday when we have more money. This trip I'll be able to sell some of the old carvings, things I did years ago."

"I don't care," she whispers, and wonders if he hears her. He turns on some horrible music, and she leans forward to switch to something else, something equally horrible.

"I love you, Elizabeth," he says.

She hums along to the music all the way, as if she can't hear him.

At last they stop at a house that's set back in a snowy garden. Elizabeth hunches her shoulders against the cold, against Pop, as Libby opens the door. She's tall, thin as a bone, peering at them with sky blue eyes behind her glasses. She's smiling, a tight smile, but still—

Good for Libby, Elizabeth thinks. She's not going to let us know what a horrible imposition this is.

Imposition. A word her English teacher, Mrs. Thomas, would love. Elizabeth feels a zing of pain in her chest. On

4

Monday she'll go to a new school where she doesn't know a soul.

They drag her duffel bags through Libby's perfect hall, into her neat living room, and Pop leans forward to kiss Elizabeth good-bye, aiming for her cheek. She pulls back and he grazes her hair.

He mumbles a few words, and then he's gone.

Blotches of red stain Libby's neck. She moves forward and reaches out to Elizabeth. A hug? But Elizabeth realizes it's her jacket Libby's after. Drops of snow are beginning to melt on the carpet.

Elizabeth has to feel sorry for Libby. She imagines Pop calling on the phone, talking Libby into taking Elizabeth, as if she's the third duffel bag.

There's another sharp zing in Elizabeth's chest. Maybe something's wrong with her heart. She catches a glimpse of herself in the mirror. Nothing's wrong with her heart, of course. Too bad. It would serve Pop right if she keeled over and stopped breathing.

She pictures it. He'd have to delay his trip while he buried her. She sees him dumping out one of the duffel bags on this shiny floor and sliding her in—

Elizabeth is alone now with Libby. What can she say to her? But Libby hoists up one of the bags, so Elizabeth takes the other one and follows Libby upstairs.

"There's just one bedroom here. Your own bathroom," Libby says. "You can read in the tub. I've put a few books on the table."

Fine. Elizabeth tells herself that she'll hide in the bathroom reading. She remembers having left the water running in the tub at home once, and later, Pop looking up at the kitchen ceiling, water dripping down from the bathroom. Pop shaking his head.

Now she and Libby stand in the doorway, and instantly Elizabeth loves the room. It's nicer than hers, nicer than her friend Alexa's. There's something cozy about it, something wonderful. If only it were really hers. The wooden floor gleams here like the one in the hall downstairs, and at the foot of the bed there's a rag rug, blue, red, and green, almost like the quilt.

Cloth houses are sewn on the quilt. They're a little crooked, but you could spend hours lying on that bed looking at those houses, pretending to open a door and walk right in.

The windows overlook the garden. It's hard to see because of all that snow mounding up over the bushes, clinging to the tree branches. A huge chair's right there at the window.

"This was my room when I was your age," Libby says. "I shared it with your mother for a while."

Her mother's room! But it's almost as if Libby's warning her not to get too fond of it. Is Libby thinking about getting her room back to herself, her house back?

Right, Elizabeth thinks.

They get through the afternoon, and dinner in the dining room, while Elizabeth keeps trying to think of things to say. At dinner the knives and forks clink loudly; she can almost hear herself and Libby chewing.

The dinner is terrible—hamburgers dry as dust, french

fries with burnt ends—but Elizabeth says, "It's the best meal I've had in a long time." And to herself, At least since breakfast.

Afterward, she and Libby watch television in the living room. Then Elizabeth sees Libby raise her hand, a fluttering motion, and Elizabeth follows Libby's eyes to the front hall. On the wall is a drawing of a girl in a sliver of a frame.

Elizabeth leans forward to get a better look. The whole thing is a mess. It's stiff with water stains and fingerprints, but worse is the girl herself. She's faded, but still you can see she wasn't pretty, not with those apple cheeks and that tiny round nose.

But Elizabeth sees what Libby wants to show her. The girl looks like Elizabeth, almost exactly like her. If Elizabeth had been wearing that cap, the kerchief crossed over her shoulders—

"Who is she?" Elizabeth asks.

"Her name was Eliza, a name like yours," Libby says. "The picture belonged to my grandmother, and her grandmother before her, and back before that. The girl was called Zee."

Elizabeth thinks, My great-grandmother, then, and her grandmother before her.

"Done on parchment. It was soft once, made from sheepskin. Zee lost—" Libby stops, her cheeks almost as red as those blotches on her neck.

There's something sad about the girl's eyes. She reminds Elizabeth of herself. "She lost her mother?"

Libby nods reluctantly.

There's more; Elizabeth can feel it. "Her father?"

"Yes, during the Revolutionary War." Libby raises her thin shoulders. "Your hair is like your mother's," she says. Changing the subject? "Shiny and straight."

Elizabeth touches her hair. Those streaks. A mistake to have tried to do them herself, she knows that.

She keeps glancing at the drawing of Zee from the living room. It's strange to look like someone who lived more than two hundred years ago. It makes her feel not quite as alone as she might be.

That night, she hunches deep under the crooked-house quilt, her head covered so Libby, downstairs in her room, can't hear her crying.

After a while, she looks toward the window at the snow drifting down. She falls asleep thinking about Eliza, called Zee. Zee, who looks like her. Zee, who seems just as sad as she is.

EIGHTEENTH CENTURY

Snowflakes like feathers! I twirled myself around in the field, mittens up, catching them, diamonds in my hands.

I turned. Mercy, the gate! How did I leave it open? Where did the sheep get to with their woolly bodies and their stringy curls?

How important those sheep were to us: food all winter, and wool for our clothes. My mouth went dry. What had I done!

I hiked up my petticoat and ran, breathless, searching. The sheep dotted the fields like mounds of snow. Who could tell the difference between them and the bushes where they sought shelter?

I stamped my feet, calling, "Weiss, Stern, Clara, where are you? Where are the rest of you?"

Not one of them came. Not one moved. The poor dumb things with their watery eyes would freeze to death.

I could imagine Father's sorrow, my brother John's anger. If only they hadn't gone to help Caleb Walker. If only Mother had returned from spinning with Mistress Patchin. I wouldn't be alone.

But I knew what I had to do.

The shame of it.

I stumbled through the drifts, which were becoming thicker, to pull the rope and sound the bell for help. It rang in my ears, deafening. It echoed across the mountains, through the valley, calling our neighbors.

I didn't wait. I ran past the henhouse, glancing toward the river with its blocks of ice, and into the back field, looking, calling, remembering how Father had walked for thirty miles to bring home the first pair of sheep years earlier.

How proud he had been of our growing farm. Small as I was, I'd listened as he'd talked about the Palatinate, the place where he and Mother had grown up near the Rhine River in Europe. "But here we came, to a new farmland, with its own river," he'd said, "and here we'll prosper."

But he'd never thought he'd have a daughter like me, who would burn the bread, ruin the fat for soap . . .

And lose the sheep.

Neighbors came from different directions: Old Gerard, the Lenape Indian, from his lean-to; Mr. Walker, with Father and John, across the back field; my best friend, Ammy, and her brother, Isaac, with the soft gray eyes, from the path through the woods.

Miller and Julian, the brothers who laughed at everything, laughed at nothing, came running. "Good men," Father always said.

The good men laughed even now, as Miller lifted me, swinging me away from the drifts. I pounded his shoulders. "Useless boy," I yelled.

He leaned forward, his face so close to mine that his thick dark hair brushed my forehead. "Who is useless, Miss Zee?"

Father heard. He turned and our eyes caught. I was sure he was thinking that I was indeed the useless girl who had caused half the valley to tramp through the snow looking for our sheep, rather than tending to their own affairs. Isaac, cheeks reddened from the cold, looked at me sympathetically.

That night, huddled under my quilt in the loft, I listened to hail pattering against the roof just over my head. Below were the crackle of the fire in the keeping room and Father's angry voice. He was talking to Mother. "What is the matter with that girl? Couldn't she take better care of the sheep?"

That girl. Me. Zee.

I longed to make him proud of me, but he was always disappointed. He'd worked so hard to carve our farm out of the wilderness; his fingers were bent from heaving rocks and tearing roots out of the soil. Father, whose rare smile warmed his face.

"We have such good neighbors to help us," Mother said. I knew she wanted him to think happier thoughts.

But as Father answered, I heard the hesitation in his voice. "We are all still friends, but our disagreements are growing stronger. Who is for the king of England? Who is against? Who wants to pay taxes for the king's last war with the French and who does not?"

For a moment there was silence. "How foolish we are," he said, "to work so hard in this colony, serving a foreign king who cares nothing for us."

Below the loft there was silence except for the snap of a pinecone in the hearth. I shivered under the quilt, my feet like blocks of ice. Stout Lucy, our cat, moved closer.

I felt hot tears on my cheeks. I had lost two of the past year's spring lambs with my forgetfulness.

Useless Zee.

elizabeth

TWENTY-FIRST CENTURY

Elizabeth walks up the front path to Libby's house and stops. She's forgotten the key. Useless, she tells herself. She can almost see the key lying on the table under the drawing of Zee.

At home, the key, tied on a ribbon, hung from a nail on the lowest branch of the evergreen in back. And even when she lost that key a couple of times, the deli was on the corner, and she could sit on a bench inside, sipping a Coke until Pop came home.

She'd watch the people coming in, guessing what their lives were like: a skinny man might be a bike racer, a plump woman would be on her way home to thump out a pie on her counter.

She closes her eyes. All this first terrible week at the new school, where she managed to lose herself on the way to social studies, and then on the way to English, she thought about the bedroom at the top of the stairs.

She can't wait to fold herself into that warm chair in front of the window and lean back into its giant pillow. She pictures herself watching the squirrels sail from branch to branch, the phoebes nesting, the pale mist of forsythia against Libby's back fence.

It's still cold, windy. Crumpled leaves skitter around, blowing into doorways. She'll have to huddle on the step, waiting until Libby gets home, like some kind of orphan.

That's not so far from the truth with Pop off somewhere in Australia, telling people about his carvings. He's e-mailed and called to tell her how much he misses her, but still it sounds as if he's having a wonderful time.

She sinks down on the brick step, feeling the cold through her jacket and jeans; even her toes feel icy. She stares at the other houses, which line both sides of the street.

After a while, she turns to look up at the window to see into that robin's egg–blue hall. It's like a warm day in there. She stares at Zee's picture, Zee warm on the wall . . .

And catches Zee's eyes. They're actually nothing but dark smudges, but it almost seems as if Zee is looking back at her, curious, interested, friendly.

Elizabeth angles her head. "Fine for you, Zee," she whispers, and then feels guilty. Zee has lost both parents and has been through a war. There's even more than that, Libby has said. But so far, Elizabeth hasn't been able to pry the story out of her; Libby barely talks.

She's really trying, though; Elizabeth knows that. This morning Libby made pancakes, thick and hard as cardboard. "Your mother loved pancakes," she said, hands fluttering. "She even ate them cold, left over, on the way to school."

Elizabeth choked down the first one. Could her mother possibly have eaten these? "Did you make pancakes for my mother?" she asked.

Libby's eyes widened. "No, our mother did. I don't really cook that well."

Together, suddenly, they were laughing, and Libby reached over, took the plate, and dumped it into the garbage. Instead, they finished off a box of raspberry Pop-Tarts. Delicious.

Elizabeth waited to hear more, but Libby glanced at her watch, rubbed her napkin across her mouth, and said, "Getting late. We have to go."

So now with nothing to do but wait for Libby to come home, Elizabeth tucks her hands into her pockets and begins to talk to Zee.

She tells Zee about sitting on the front steps of her house in Middletown, watching her father paint the door with careful stripes of the brush. It was a hideous gray. "Why not red?" she asked him. "Or peach?"

He grunted.

"Why not?"

He finally answered. "I had this paint left over in the garage."

"It's horrible," she said, imagining that her mother was alive and painting the door a creamy yellow. Without thinking, she leaned back on her elbows and knocked over the paint can.

She scrambled to put the can upright, her hands sticky with paint. But as Pop watched the thick paint flowing down from the top step to the next, he just shook his head. "Think!"

She finishes telling the story to Zee. There are a dozen

other things she might talk about as well: losing her mother's silver ring; wishing she had a dog she'd name Elliot; her new homeroom teacher, Mrs. Sparks, who licks her lips before she speaks, a dreadful habit.

Elizabeth stares at the drawing. Zee looks so much like her. It's almost as if she's found a friend to talk to.

She can't wait to find out more from Libby. She wants to gather together every single scrap Libby knows about Zee; she wants to know Zee.

And here comes Libby in her small car. She hurries up the front path, keys in her hand.

"I forgot the key," Elizabeth says, shrugging a little.

Libby shakes her head.

It reminds Elizabeth of Pop. It's a wonder Libby doesn't say think. It's good, too, that Libby doesn't know she's been sitting there, talking to a picture.

She'd think Elizabeth was crazy.

So would Pop.

EIGHTEENTH CENTURY

Over my head, oak leaves lined the branches like furry mouse ears.

"It's the time to plant," Old Gerard had told Ammy Patchin and me as he'd sifted corn kernels through his leathery fingers. Old Gerard, the Lenape, knew all about those things. So that's what Ammy and I were doing:

Poking a stick into the earth.

Dropping three kernels into the hole.

Whispering, "Be happy down there."

No, Ammy wasn't whispering to the corn. Ammy didn't talk to things the way I did, didn't tell the bread to rise, the sun to come out. But she always met me, running, halfway across the field when our chores were done.

"Cold," I said to her today; I was shivering.

"Windy," she agreed.

We watched a few sad leaves from last fall skitter across the field. My cap wanted to fly off my head, but I held on to it. In the next field, my brother John's jacket flapped around him. It looked as if he'd sail away across the mountains.

And I was without the woolly shawl I had knitted last winter. Where was it? I wrinkled my forehead. Maybe it had been captured by a thornbush, or floated down the river to see the world. Imagine. A red shawl with dropped stitches curtsying to King George or Queen Charlotte. I had to laugh at my foolishness.

Hands tapped my cheeks. Ammy, smelling like lavender, leaned over. "It's worse to laugh to yourself, Zee."

"Worse than what?" But then I waved my hand. "Never mind. I know. Worse than talking to—"

"Yourself," Ammy said, but she said it kindly. We locked arms to look at our corn patch. The rows zigzagged along, looking like my hair when it was newly plaited.

Father and Mr. Patchin had given us this square of land as soon as Ammy and I had been old enough to plant. It was no bigger than our keeping room. Half of it was on Father's land, half on Mr. Patchin's. Once, they had been best friends, like Ammy and me. But that had been before all this talk of war.

Don't think about that, Zee, I told myself. I might as well have said it aloud, because Ammy knew what was in my mind. Her eyes floated in tears.

I bent over to poke in another hole, humming so she'd think everything was all right. But it wasn't all right. Trouble was coming upon us like a twist of clouds just before the streak of lightning seared the earth.

Last night John had pounded the table until the plates had jumped. "There will be war," he'd said. "And after planting I will go to fight against the Loyalists."

War. I had run my finger over a bit of spilled soup and brought it to my mouth. Warm. Salty. Don't think about war.

Father opened his mouth. I thought it was to scold John. But no. He looked serious, his slate blue eyes darker than usual. "It will come to that for us both." He shook his head. "Neighbor against neighbor. The Loyalists will fight for the king; others like us will fight to be free."

Now John came across the field, a hoe in one hand, his face like thunder. He held his hat against the wind, glaring at Ammy: Ammy in her soft cap with the red ribbon, Ammy with her turned-up nose. Who could be angry at her?

"Where's your brother?" John asked. "Where's Isaac?"

Ammy barely looked up. "I don't know."

"He's off doing mischief with the Loyalists. Maybe he's in Canada with Colonel St. Leger. They say St. Leger's coming down the St. Lawrence. We've all heard that. He'll meet up with General Burgoyne, and squeeze New York until there's not an American left to fight." He squeezed the end of his jacket, his knuckles white.

Ammy straightened herself. Two spots of red circled her cheeks. "Loyalty to King George is not mischief. This country belongs to him, belongs to England."

I thought John would burst with anger. He bent down and gripped a clump of earth in his fist. "The king has never seen this soil, never touched foot on this land. He cares only about taking what we have, our money in taxes, our food, our animal skins."

There was no other sound then except the whooshing of the wind. John crumbled the soil in his hand. "It's your brother, Isaac, who is the traitor," he told her.

Isaac, a traitor? I pictured his smile that was only for me. Isaac, whom I hoped to wed someday.

I turned away from John's angry face and looked at the river. The waves were like small white horses prancing north, prancing to where the fighting might be.

Soil and pebbles rattled as John threw the dirt across the field.

He looked toward Ammy's cabin, hidden by the trees. "House of our enemies," he said.

He left us and went back to the field. He stood there, hands on his hips, shoulders heaving.

Tears streamed down Ammy's face. John had never talked to her like that.

My own tears came. When John made up his mind, there was no changing it. And deep inside my head was a voice that whispered, this time Father agreed with him.

"When the corn grows a little," Ammy said, "we will plant the beans. They will use the cornstalks as poles to hold themselves up."

I took a breath. "And then the squash," I said, my voice even. "It will grow in the shade of its two sisters, the corn and the beans."

We were using Old Gerard's words about planting. They never changed. But think of how his life had changed! After having lived here for hundreds of years, the Lenapes had lost all their land to the Iroquois and left for the West. Only Gerard and his grandson remained, in his lean-to.

That last day, his daughter had gathered her children around her, falling to her knees, begging Gerard to come with them.

He'd answered her slowly. "I stay out of respect to the old

ones. Their spirits have gone to the sky, but their bones remain. Who else is there to care about them but me?"

She'd walked across the field, her children following. Then she'd turned. "Stay with your grandfather, Elam."

Elam kept plodding along until his mother picked up some small stones and threw them at his feet. Then, at last, he started back and I saw that he was smiling. Staying with his grandfather was what he wanted after all.

Now Ammy touched my shoulder. "By the time we harvest the corn, we will have forgotten this talk of war." Her face was set, determined.

Please, I told myself. Ammy is right more times than not. Let her be right now.

EIGHTEENTH CENTURY

The rain began late one night. It spattered hard on the roof: an angry sound against the logs, the chunks of clay, and the chimney stones.

Stout Lucy, the cat, hated it. She curled herself up on the quilt next to my feet. I thought of the likeness of Lucy that was lying near my pallet. It had been drawn on a mushroom with a nail, and showed her irritable face. That cat was always angry.

I couldn't sleep. Was it because I had forgotten something? What was it? Not the sheep. I had closed their gate, so it wasn't that. Why did I picture Miller standing on top of our henhouse, nails in his mouth, hammer in his hand, the day our neighbors had built it together?

And then I knew. The henhouse!

I climbed down from the loft, and in the glow of the banked fireplace ashes, I let myself out without a sound. Old Gerard had taught me that—to watch my footsteps, to tread carefully. "Important for the hunter," he'd said.

I ducked my head against the storm. Facing me was the river, the shallows white against the rocks, and the center pockmarked with fierce drops. Beyond the rushing water were the fields, green now, but beaten down.

Closer was the chicken coop. The door swung back and forth, banging; the rope that usually held it fast lay loose. My fist went to my mouth. I had fed the hens and given them water but had forgotten to close them in for the night.

How thankful I was that I'd discovered it before Mother or Father had. But then I saw puffs of white: my poor hens skittering over the mud. An animal with matted fur held a hen in its jaws.

I picked up a rock and sent it after the creature, but with the rain in my eyes, my aim was poor. The fox disappeared around the side of the coop, its thick tail almost sweeping the ground.

A footfall sounded behind me. Hands covered my mouth and my nose, hands that made it hard to breathe. I felt as if I were a hen in the jaws of the fox. I arched my back and brought my hands up to his wrists, scratching wildly.

"Be still, Zee." The hands came away from my face and clamped on my arms.

John.

"You might have killed me," I said.

His wet hands tightened on my arms. "Ah, Zee, I didn't want you to wake Mother."

"We have to capture the hens." I leaned against him in spite of myself and wiped my eyes and my cheeks.

"Never mind the hens just yet," he said.

I shook my head. The fox would be back sooner or later. He'd take not only a hen but what that hen would give us—an egg a day and eventually a meal on the table.

John moved me forward to stand under the shelter of the trees. "You might as well know," he said. "I'm leaving now with Miller and his brother Julian before Mother sees me. I can't bear to see her tears."

Leaving? In the rain? In the middle of the night? Oh, John and Julian. Oh, Miller. Annoying as Miller was, he'd helped furrow our fields and mill our grain.

I grasped John's sleeve. "Why would you do that?"

"I have to fight," he said.

I looked up at him. His hat was soaked with rain, the drops rolling off the edge. In the dim light, it was hard to see his eyes. "War is not here," I said. "It hasn't come to us."

"Oh, Zee." His voice was harsh. "We'll all be pulled in before long. This is about being free to live our own lives."

"I'm free enough!"

"Father and I have been outspoken against the king, and there are Loyalists here who want us gone."

I thought of the Patchins. "We'll always live one field away," Ammy had said. "We'll sugar together in the spring; we'll quilt all winter." And Isaac, perching on the fence he was supposed to be mending, patting the rough wood with his freckled hand, and saying, "Put down your basket, Zee. We'll sit awhile."

Isaac.

I must have said it aloud, because John repeated bitterly, "Isaac. He's gone off to fight with the Loyalists. And there are others in this valley who would fight, too. We left them a warning, Miller and Julian and I."

I shook my head as John grabbed my arm. "They'll try to hurt us, all of them, the British and the Loyalists."

It was too much to think about. "Don't go, John." I wrung my hands. "Suppose something happens to you?"

"I'll go north," he said, as if I hadn't spoken. He pointed over his shoulder.

"No need to point," I said. I knew well where the sun came up, and where it disappeared at night. To go north, he'd have to keep the sun on his right in the morning, on his left in the afternoon.

"I heard about a militia," John said. "I'll train up near Fort Dayton with General Herkimer."

A name so strange I could hardly say it.

"Herkimer's father came from the Palatinate in Europe, like Father," he said. "One of our own."

Inside the house a light flickered. Father must be awake. I turned to John, but he had moved into the trees. And in moments it seemed as if he had melted away. Old Gerard had taught him well, too.

I looked at the trunks darkened by rain, the leaves dripping. But I couldn't stand there for long. I had to take care of the sodden hens. I flapped my petticoat, trying to guide them into the coop. I clucked at them gently. Poor hens. Their feathers were bedraggled, weighed down with mud. There would be no keeping this from Father.

But all I could think of was John, remembering games we had played together when we were young, remembering that he'd carried me home when I had twisted my ankle, that he'd shared food with me in lean times.

I looped the rope over the coop door and made sure it was closed tight, then went toward the house.

Father stood in front, peering at me. "Zee?"

I stood still, afraid to move, the rain coming down at me. "I am sorry about the hens."

"The hens?"

"A fox got one of them."

He took a step forward, too angry to speak.

"And John is gone," I said, wanting to distract him.

His face changed. "I knew he'd go. If it weren't for the farm, if it weren't for Mother, I would go, too."

I felt a pain deep in my chest. Father was stern, but I loved his spareness, his gentle handling of the animals. I was glad the farm and Mother would hold him back.

Inside, Mother sat at the table, her head bowed in her hands. "I know it's John," she said.

I poured cider into mugs and put one in front of her. She cupped her hands around it. "You're a good child, Zee."

I glanced at Father. I was not a good child. We might lose our hens to the chill because of my forgetfulness. And now that John was gone, how could I take his place? I had little strength to be of real help to Father in the fields.

As for helping Mother, I tangled the yarn in the spinning

wheel; my stitches were uneven when we sewed petticoats or shirts. I burned mush in the pots, and cakes in their iron forms. Now I took a sip of the warm cider and held its sweetness in my mouth.

I had to do better.

I had to try.

TWENTY-FIRST CENTURY

After yesterday's breakfast of almost raw eggs and burnt bacon, Libby shook her head. "I'm giving up cooking in the morning."

"That's a relief," Elizabeth blurted out, thinking of the times they've eaten together: soggy French toast, waffles hard as rocks. Then, horrified at what she'd said, she'd patted Libby's arm to make up for it.

Libby laughed. "You remind me so much of your mother."

Elizabeth knew Libby was saying it as a compliment. It gave her a warm syrupy feeling.

This morning she stands in the hall, the last of her toast in one hand, a glass of apple juice in the other. She's whispering to Zee's drawing. If only Zee could step out of her frame, alive and breathing, Elizabeth would never need another friend.

What would Libby think about her talking to a picture?

What would the kids in her class say? They haven't talked much to her in the month she's been here, but actually, she hasn't talked to them much, either.

Every day at lunchtime she sits on the end of a bench, any bench at any table, and pretends to study her sandwich, her milk container. Sometimes she reads. Nobody notices her.

She feels a hot flush of embarrassment when she thinks about a field trip her history class took. Mr. Stewart had them wandering around the muddy Catskills searching for arrowheads, obsidian, and mica and wading into the west branch of the Delaware for smooth bits of glass. He was in love with the past.

Elizabeth found a small sparkling rock and held it up, picturing a comet exploding, far up, worlds away, a shower of hot golden colors raining down on the earth, and now one of those pieces, cool and smooth, lay in the palm of her hand.

"If only I hadn't said all that aloud," she tells Zee. At home she wouldn't have been embarrassed. Even Pop would have nodded seriously. That's Elizabeth, they all would have said.

But here everyone looked away as Mr. Stewart explained that it was a petrified chunk of wood from a tree that had fallen long ago.

Elizabeth stares at Zee's face. Her hands are hidden. Elizabeth knows about that now.

Last night she cornered Libby in the small study. Libby's back was to the door as she read from a large notebook. She looked up, tilting the book. "Part of my research," she said.

"I'm always at it, even most weekends. Studying bacteria. What makes them survive, what makes them die off."

Elizabeth nodded, then sat on the couch opposite her, leaning forward, hands on her knees. "I want to know about Zee."

Libby put down her book. "All we know are bits and pieces, passed down for so many years." She hesitated. "Her hands were badly burned."

Elizabeth felt her breath catch.

"Their cabin was set on fire and it burned to the ground. Only a few stones were left to mark where it had been. Her mother—" Libby shook her head.

"Burned?" Elizabeth asks, her voice strangled.

"She was killed, maybe by Loyalists who lived in the valley, maybe by Indians. No one ever knew."

How soft Libby's eyes were; Elizabeth realized Libby cared about what had happened to Zee. Elizabeth pictured flames shooting up, exploding into orange embers. How frightened Zee must have been, and how terrible the pain. How had Zee escaped? And what about her father? Had he been there to beat out the flames, to wrap her hands?

Or had she been alone?

Elizabeth remembered one night when she was four, or maybe five. She'd been alone upstairs in her bedroom. Pop had been carving one of his art things in the basement. He carved unusual pieces; it was hard to make sense of them. She'd heard a sound, and then another. Footsteps on the stairs? The third step always creaked. She'd pulled the blanket off her bed and silently, slowly opened the closet door and bundled herself inside.

But no one had been there. Pop had come up later, making so much noise on the stairs that she'd known he was real.

Pop, who was miles away.

❦

This morning Elizabeth stares at Zee's picture. Zee, with the terrible burned hands.

Elizabeth tells herself it was more than two hundred years ago, trying not to care so much.

She wants to think of something else. Anything else. She looks at the cap with the ruffled edges Zee has plopped down over her head, her hair escaping in many directions.

At least Elizabeth washes her hair every morning—two rinses, conditioner, and gel. She doesn't have to wear a cap because her hair hasn't seen a bucket of water or a cake of soap in months. That's what Libby told her about those caps. And what about the soap! In those days they poured boiling water over ashes and mixed in animal fat.

Pretty awful.

Elizabeth winds a thin strand of hair around her finger. Mr. Stewart has asked them to bring in something old today. "The oldest thing you can find. An artifact from the past," he said.

Elizabeth looks up at the drawing. Who could doubt that it's old? How could a grandfather's blackthorn cane compare, or a pair of candlesticks that belong to someone's mother?

She's thinking of taking the drawing to school. She can ask, but what if Libby says no?

Not even *what if*. She's sure Libby will say no. She can

imagine Libby shaking her head, her blue eyes blinking behind her glasses.

But Libby works in a lab across town; Elizabeth might be able to get the picture back up on the wall before she gets home.

And if not?

That's late this afternoon. She won't worry about it yet. By the end of the day, she'll have her first A in Mr. Stewart's history class.

And maybe the kids in her class will see her—she tries to think of the word—*differently*.

She unhooks the drawing from the wall and slides it into her backpack.

Libby calls, "Want a lift?"

Elizabeth glances toward the window. It's warm today, and the apple tree is veiled in white, like a bride. A few flowers drift to the ground, the train of its gown.

"Elizabeth," Libby calls.

Elizabeth shakes her head. How guilty she'd feel knowing the drawing was in the car with them. Suppose Libby could tell by her face, by her eyes, that she'd done something—something just not right.

"I'll walk," she says.

EIGHTEENTH CENTURY

I walked to the edge of the river and bent over to dab water on my face. I had to be careful to keep my clean cap dry. I hurried. Mother wouldn't approve of my being there alone.

"This is a smaller river than our Rhine River in Europe, but often it brings trouble," she'd say. "Illness, angry Iroquois, thieves, poachers, and . . ." Her voice would trail off.

Was she thinking ghosts or English? I couldn't decide which.

I was drawn to the river Old Gerard called Big Fish Water. I loved watching whiskered catfish sweep slowly along the sandy bottom, pickerel and bass moving silently just under the surface. Often I sneaked up on turtles sunning themselves on the rocks, but I never reached them before they disappeared into the water.

I wrapped my arms around myself. Even though the coming day would be warm, the water on my face was icy. "A good morning for catching trout," Gerard would say.

But I was on my way to see Ammy's mother, Mistress Patchin, without Father's knowing. Mistress Patchin had a face like their watchdog's, and was just as unfriendly. But I had to help her make soap. Then she'd cut off a block of it for me to take to Mother. "We must ask because we have none," Mother had said, shaking her head.

We both knew it was my fault. Hadn't I left the door open so the ashes flew into the wind? Hadn't I spilled the bucket of fat that spread itself into thick puddles on the doorstep and mingled with mud and hen droppings?

Now I scooped up another handful of water for my face. I waited for the river to settle. Waited to see myself.

My eyes were the color of the river on a cloudy day. My nose was small and round, and freckles dotted my cheeks like spots on a trout. "Good morning, Zee," I told myself kindly.

Zee smiled back at me.

Isaac Patchin liked my face; I knew that.

I patted the water until my face wrinkled up and was gone.

Soap for Mother, I reminded myself. And Father will never know where it came from.

I didn't mind going to the Patchins' farm, even though Mistress Patchin had slapped my poor speckled cheeks when I'd left her gate open and the hog had run loose.

I climbed up from the river, rubbed my water-wrinkled fingers on my petticoat, then picked up the hard bread Mother had wrapped for my meal.

I had a long way to walk, but I paid it no mind. The path wound its way through the apple trees and curved through Old Gerard's planting field. I picked through my thoughts the way I worried nut meats from their shells in the fall. I had time to think about which of our neighbors were Loyalists. The Patchins, of course.

I wondered about our other neighbors. Certainly not Miller and Julian, who were off with John to the north. Certainly not Old Gerard, who said he had given up fighting long before I was born.

Nor Mistress Eddy, whose face was as creased as the river in a storm, and whose lips trembled with age.

What about the others? The Williams family, whose house hung on the side of the mountain, threatening to slide down any minute? Or the Gregorys, who kept to themselves? And there were families who lived in the next valley and those who perched in tents at the edge of the river.

I turned with the path at the cornfield. Overhead a hawk screeched. A rabbit zigzagged away, trying for safety, but there was no place for the poor thing to hide.

I wondered at my pity. After all, I was always the first one to scoop rabbit stew into my bowl and to lick every one of my fingers for a last taste.

But this rabbit looked terrified. Its ears were laid back and its body hugged the ground as it ran, almost as if it could sink into the earth. I screamed at the hawk, waving my arms.

The rabbit reached the rocks just before the hawk swooped. Safe.

But I was as unfortunate as the hungry hawk. I stumbled and went down hard. My cheek scraped a stone, my sleeve tore as the hawk dived over the rocks and plucked up a snake. It flew over the trees with the snake dangling from its beak like a twisted rope.

I sat up, rubbing my elbow, trying to straighten my cap. I touched my cheek carefully. How could I face Mistress Patchin looking this way?

I saw Old Gerard come out of his lean-to. He stood against the trunk of the tree that bent over his doorway, and cupped his hand over his eyes. "Zee?"

I hobbled over to him. We sat ourselves on a smooth rock, me to catch my breath, and Gerard to put his leathery face to the sun. His eyes were the color of walnuts that appeared in the tree over our heads each fall, and the lines around his eyes were like crevices. His grandson Elam came outside their small lean-to, which backed up against a hill, closing the makeshift door behind him. The three of us sat there peacefully, listening to the sad coo of a mourning dove.

The sun had shifted. How long had I been there? A few minutes? It must have been longer.

I scrambled up. "I have to go." I shook the dust from my petticoat and ran. As I reached the woods, stones and small brown twigs dug into my bare feet.

At the Patchins' fence posts, I had to stop. Bent over, I took in deep gulps of breath, my hands on my knees, my chest heaving. I plucked my cap into shape, rubbed one foot against the other, then straightened my kerchief.

In front of me was the Patchins' finely made house, wider than ours. It had glass windows. Glass instead of oiled paper!

Ammy's family was rich. Hadn't I seen Mistress Patchin hide a gold coin on top of the shelf near the hearth? I had lowered my eyes that day so she wouldn't know I was watching.

Their door was open, swung back, and a slip of paper was stabbed into it with a knife. I looked closely at the letters, but I didn't recognize most of the words. I knew, though, that it was the warning John had left for them.

I poked my head in. "It's Zee," I called, blinking in the dim light. The old chair that Mistress Patchin prized was tipped over, and strands of Mistress Patchin's brown wool were bunched up on the floor like a small bird. I stepped inside. The ashes in the fireplace were cool. I ran my hand over the shelf. The coin was gone, but the wooden plates were still on the table, a bit of food left in each.

How could this be? I was shocked at Mistress Patchin. The plates should have been brushed out and put up on the shelf.

The bedding was gone, and the spider pan missing from its hook. I tried to take it all in. What could have happened?

The Patchins were gone.

TWENTY-FIRST CENTURY

The class crowds around Elizabeth, and Mr. Stewart does, too.

"How old is the drawing?" That's what he wants to know. He runs his fingers over the frame and taps the glass gently. "The cap," he says almost as if he's talking to himself. "Could it possibly be eighteenth century?"

"Revolutionary War days," Elizabeth says.

The kids are looking at her; Karen points. "She looks a little—"

Elizabeth raises her hand to her face. "Like me."

"A lot," Annie says, and for the first time, she smiles at Elizabeth.

Elizabeth smiles back, then looks down at the picture.

Zee's cap, the long strands of hair across her cheek, the kerchief that covers her shoulders and crosses in front are all different from the way Elizabeth looks. Nothing like her streaked hair, her hoodie, her jeans.

Except for one thing.

No matter how often Elizabeth combs her hair or wears a new sweater, she ends up looking as messy as Zee does. She wishes she could reach out and put her arms around that long-ago Zee.

Mr. Stewart doesn't look up; he can't take his eyes off the drawing. "Notice the glass. It's not flat; it curves out just a little."

He looks at Elizabeth. "Someone in your family put it together, maybe a hundred years ago." His smile is warm and approving. "To keep it safe for the future. That would be you, Elizabeth."

"She was in a fire," Elizabeth says slowly.

Everyone looks more closely.

Zee's face is untouched. So are her clothes.

"Her hands were burned." Elizabeth holds up her own hands. "Her skin must have been webbed, her fingernails thickened. She couldn't have touched anything, lifted anything, not for weeks. . . ." Her voice trails off.

Around her, the kids are nodding. They look at the drawing a little longer, everyone quiet.

"Wonderful," Mr. Stewart says. "Thank you for bringing this in."

Annie taps the glass. "You could see it better if you took it out of the frame."

Elizabeth looks at her in alarm. What will she do if Mr. Stewart agrees? Suppose they can't get Zee back inside the frame again.

She shakes her head, and at the same time, Mr. Stewart's eyes widen. "We can't do that; the glass and frame protect it." He holds the picture in both hands. "Don't you see?

That's why we have so little of the past. We don't take care of the things that remain."

Annie puts her hand on Elizabeth's shoulder. "Sorry," she says. Then she adds, "How about sitting with Merry and me at lunch?"

"Sure," Elizabeth says as Annie opens a box.

"I brought my mother's wedding gloves," Annie says. She pulls them out and waves the fingers. "But that was only fifteen years ago."

The bell rings. On her way to her locker, Elizabeth looks out the window next to the stairs. She watches a bird flit from one tree to another. A robin, maybe.

Still holding the picture, she goes downstairs. She has kids to sit with, and it's all because of Zee. She likes having this locker. At home, there are hooks for jackets in the hallways instead; uneven piles of books and lunch bags cascade out from underneath.

Elizabeth twirls the lock: twenty-fourteen-two, then a twist to the right. The lock sticks as she tries to pull it open with one hand.

The picture slips out of her other hand and falls to the floor. The narrow frame cracks, and the glass shatters in an arc around her feet. The backing hits her foot, and the drawing sails across the tile floor.

A couple of kids stand there, mouths open. Elizabeth thinks she might be sick.

She kneels down to pick up the drawing, feeling a sharp pain as a piece of glass embeds itself in her knee.

She takes the drawing gently between her thumb and index finger, almost afraid to look. Please, she thinks. Please.

And there's Zee, up close, looking at her. She's sharper, clearer, outside the frame.

"All right?" one of the kids says nervously.

She looks up and nods.

Pop's face flashes into her mind, and then she feels a sudden panic. She hasn't seen Libby angry. Libby is . . .

It's hard to describe. Steady, maybe. Libby smiles, but she doesn't laugh. She speaks slowly, quietly. But suppose that's just one side of Libby. Suppose she's furious when she sees this. Suppose she puts Elizabeth out.

Where could she go? Hitchhike back to her empty house in Middletown? Break in through a window? Live there by herself until Pop came back?

She leans back against the wall. There's a round red stain on her jeans.

"Don't move," Annie says. "Let me get some help."

So she sits there, wondering how she's ever going to tell Libby, while the custodian sweeps up the frame and the glass that someone put together for the future.

She holds the drawing on her lap and turns it over. On the back she sees a group of uneven lines. In one corner are three triangles, the one in the center larger than the other two. Up a little farther are intersecting bits, curling around themselves.

What is it? What could it mean?

Mr. Stewart comes along and gives her a hand up. He helps her wrap the drawing. And all the time, she's thinking, Libby.

What will she say to Libby?

What will Libby say to her?

EIGHTEENTH CENTURY

I started home from the Patchins' place along the river's edge, walking softly in the mud. I was mindful of disturbing the kingfisher that was balanced on a hollow log and the purple finches that flitted along the willow branches, chattering to each other.

But why was I watching the birds? It would have been better for me to think of what I'd say to Mother. How could I ease her disappointment when she saw me returning without soap?

The kingfisher flew up suddenly, and I realized the finches had stopped their chirping.

It was almost as if Old Gerard stood in front of me, hand up, warning me. Someone was coming—someone who didn't care about the noise. Twigs crackled and small stones pinged as they

47

were dislodged. Ghosts weren't about in the daylight, but I slipped back into the trees and held myself completely still. I heard the sound of someone's hard breath, and whoever it was stumbled past me.

"Ammy!"

She reached out to me to steady herself. "I'm so glad it's you," she said when she could talk. The hem of her petticoat was wet, her sleeves were muddy, and her hair had escaped from her cap. "I was coming to find you, but I have only a moment."

I reached out absently to wipe a spot of mud from her cheek.

"Father has gone ahead," she said, "and Mother has stopped for something at Mistress Eddy's cabin."

"I was late this morning," I said, trying to make sense of it all. "When will we make soap?"

"Zee! Look at me." Her face was the color of old milk. "I've come to tell you. You must leave, or you'll be hurt."

I ran my tongue over my lips. What was she talking about?

"The Loyalists are massing together; they're determined to put an end to this rebellion." She raised my chin with her finger. "And your family—"

"We're Americans," I said slowly, finding the words John used over and over. "And this is our country."

"No," she said. "We're on British soil, and those who deny it are nothing but—" She hesitated. "John and his friends left frightful messages at the Loyalists' doors. And those who are true to the king won't stand for it."

I stared at her. She looked almost wild.

"The Loyalists have the power," she said. "The Iroquois have come in on our side."

I felt a tremor in my fingers, my chin quivering.

"My father wants no part of this fight," she said. "We are going to Ticonderoga, and then to Canada. A terrible journey, but we'll be safe there, away from all this." She stopped, her own chin unsteady. "Tell your father." She waved one hand uncertainly. "Find safety."

She gave me a little push, then turned and was gone, splashing through the mud along the riverbank.

How long did I stand there, frozen in that spot? It was enough time for the chatter of the birds to begin again and the kingfisher to swoop back onto his log.

I ran from the riverbank, taking the old Lenape trail that wound through the trees. Only at the edge of Old Gerard's field did I stop to gasp for breath.

Gerard stood at the far end. He waved, and I raised my hand, but I kept going, running across the field, climbing over the rocks near the river, looking for Father.

I burst into the house after circling Stout Lucy, who was sunning herself on the stones in front. Mother stood there silently, shaking her head as I began to speak.

"Zee," she said, "what you have to say will have to wait. There's something I must tell you first." Her eyes filled with tears. "Your father has gone north to Tryon County to prepare for battle with Herkimer's men."

There was that name again: Herkimer.

"General Herkimer's father came from nearby in the Old Country." She took a breath. "Father said he cannot wait, he cannot stay, he has to be part of this fight. If we don't win, we'll lose everything, house and land, maybe even—" She stopped, biting off her words the way she'd bite off a strand of sewing thread.

"We've spent our days together, your father and I. How strange to be without him now." She waved her hand toward the table. "I told him I couldn't bear not to know where he was, and so he left us this."

A piece of parchment lay on the table, a map drawn with walnut ink. The lines led to Father, to John. The lines led to Herkimer.

"Keep it, child," Mother said. "It's a piece of Father. I have it in my head now, in my heart."

I picked it up and held it in my hands. Then I tucked it under my kerchief to keep it safe.

I sank onto the one chair in front of the hearth, trying to take everything in. "Ammy says that the Loyalists will come after us," I said finally, "that they'll hurt us."

She didn't answer.

"The Iroquois have joined them."

I saw her look of fear, but her voice was calm. "And the British regulars are not far away, I suppose," she said. "But we will go on as we have been. There is nothing else we can do."

And so that was what we did. I picked up the yarn that had been dyed, and began to knit a sock. Knit one, purl one, knit one—

I lost a stitch and watched it travel down three or four rows before I caught it with the edge of my needle.

Mother prepared the pans for cheese making and then began a supper of bread and a few early strawberries.

The only sound we heard as the sky darkened into evening was the snapping of logs in the fireplace. We listened, waiting for something else.

TWENTY-FIRST CENTURY

Waiting is so hard. How is she ever going to tell Libby? She walks home from school, the packaged drawing under her arm. She remembers a book Pop read to her: *It was the best of times, it was the worst of times.*

That was today. At school Annie and two other girls went with her to the nurse's office. They stayed while the nurse slapped bandages on her knee. Then Annie made room for her at the lunch table. If anyone had told her a week ago—even three days ago—that she'd have friends here, she wouldn't have believed it.

Suppose she just leaves the drawing on Libby's dining room table. Suppose she packs up a few things—not two heavy duffel bags' worth, of course. She sees herself at the entrance to the highway a few blocks away, raising her thumb. Dangerous. She could never do it.

How many miles is it to home?

She thinks of Pop. When he e-mails her, she doesn't e-mail back. She barely speaks when he calls. If she'd been home, she would never have gotten into this mess!

She realizes she's been standing under a sycamore for the past several minutes. A woman is peering at her from her window.

She begins to run, her backpack bouncing gently. But as she turns the last corner, she sees the blue car in the driveway. Her mouth goes dry. Libby is home early.

Elizabeth walks up the front path, pulls out her key, and lets herself inside. Is Libby in the kitchen? In a corner of the living room? Everything is quiet, except for a tiny ping coming from the faucet in the kitchen.

She lays the drawing on the dining room table. Then she climbs up to the bedroom and throws herself into the chair. She sinks into the pillows, wishing she could stay there forever. She glances at the quilt with its crooked houses and picks a green one. She pretends it belongs to her, that she's sitting on the porch reading a great book. Inside, Pop would be carving a small animal, or a bird. Neither of them would have ever heard of Australia.

Outside, movement catches her eye. She leans forward to see that several dead branches have been piled up in a corner of the yard. Libby is raking furiously, her face red under a wide straw gardening hat.

Elizabeth watches her; has Libby seen the empty space? Does she know the drawing is gone?

Elizabeth ducks back in the chair, just to be sure Libby won't look up and see her.

What can she say? What can she possibly say? Why has

she done this terrible thing, anyway? Think, Pop would have said.

Libby glances up. Her eyes look worried, or maybe sad.

Libby must be able to see her. Elizabeth raises her hand to wave.

Libby pushes her hat back and motions for her to come down.

Elizabeth walks to the stairs and looks back at the room. If only she could stop time and hold on to this moment, seeing this wonderful bedroom, the quilt with its crooked houses.

She goes downstairs slowly, then through the kitchen, tightening the faucet. How will she explain?

But she doesn't have to explain to Libby yet; she doesn't have to say a word. Libby says, "Hi! Can you help me with the winter branches?"

They drag the branches out to the back and lean against the fence, winded.

"Elizabeth," Libby begins, and stops.

Elizabeth looks away. "I'm sorry," she says in a voice so low she wonders if Libby can hear her. "I took the picture of Zee. I broke the glass, the frame. I've ruined everything."

"Your father called," Libby says, as if she hasn't even heard Elizabeth.

Elizabeth tries to connect this. Libby has seen that the picture is missing? She's told Pop? And Pop—what?

Libby rushes on. "I've lived alone for such a long time."

"I should never have taken it." Elizabeth's eyes are so filled with tears that it's hard to see. Libby's eyes seem blurred to her, but soft behind her glasses.

Libby reaches out and touches Elizabeth's cheek; she runs her hand over Elizabeth's hair. "Poor child," she says, as if she's the one who has to be sorry about what has happened.

For the first time, Elizabeth realizes what it must be like to have a mother. How wonderful it would be. If only she could do everything over, she'd be perfect—so perfect Libby would never want her to leave.

"Having you to look after was such a shock," Libby says. "Not being able to read at dinnertime, trying to talk, having to cook meals when I'm the worst cook—"

"You're not so bad," Elizabeth says automatically. Libby couldn't be much worse. But what difference does it make? She knows what's coming, knows that Libby is trying to tell her she can't stay.

And that's exactly what Libby says. "Your father is coming home early. He called an hour ago. He's finished in Australia. He said to tell you he's sold all the carvings, even the miserable ones." Libby stops. It's as if she can't get the words out. "He'll pick you up on Monday."

Elizabeth thinks of leaving Libby, leaving Zee. Her mind goes to the chess set in the living room that she's never tried, to lunchtime today, to swapping stories with Annie.

She stares down at the branches and the few crumpled leaves that still cling to them. She hears a woodpecker knocking at the oak tree in back of them and a mourning dove cooing its sad song.

She hears something else. Libby is making a sound in her throat.

"I've wanted to tell you," Libby says, "that my life has

changed since you've been here. I hurry home after work, and—" She reaches out and wraps her skinny arms around Elizabeth.

Elizabeth is used to Pop's hugs, but this is different, softer, a little awkward because she's not used to it. Was her mother skinny like this? Would her arms have felt the same way?

She's going to lose all this, her new life with Libby.

"I argued with your father," Libby says. "I told him you're happy here, I'm happy. I've asked him to let you stay for a while and finish the term at school. But he says he misses you. He needs you."

Elizabeth looks up.

"Of course he misses you," Libby says. "Who wouldn't?" She pauses. "I didn't tell him that we both love Zee. I didn't tell him we both talk to her." She nods. "I've heard you."

Elizabeth is really crying now. She feels as if she's going to choke.

"The first time I talked to Zee," Libby says, "I was exactly your age." She takes a breath, crying, too. "You're so much like your mother, Elizabeth."

Libby's hair smells shampoo clean, and the plants against the fence are green. If only she'd never come here, she wouldn't know what it was like.

"If I know anything," Libby says, "I know that Zee would have loved you. Don't worry about the picture. We'll get a new frame, and a piece of glass. That's not so terrible." And then she stops. "What will I do without you?"

EIGHTEENTH CENTURY

The days passed, warm days, waiting days. Everything was alive; there were mud nests of barn swallows over the doorway, eels in the river, woodpeckers hammering, frogs peeping at night from the trees, their music so loud the whole world hummed with it.

I remembered one year; a wren had fallen from its nest. Isaac had held me up, the bird cupped in my hand, to bring it back to its frantic mother.

Where was Isaac now?

Where were John and Father?

How hard it was to be alone, Mother and I going about our work quietly, watching, listening.

I had a new thought. It began as I looked at the land around me; the sturdy corn in neat rows; the herb garden that Mother tended, bending, her face red with effort; the house that Father had built with his own hands.

Did I not have a part in that building? I had helped fill in the spaces between the logs so that inside we'd be snug and warm. I'd brought hay to the cow and milked her in the mornings. I'd helped with the birthing of the lambs.

Our land, our food, our house. Not the king's.

I felt that even more when I pulled open the door that led to the root cellar. At the bottom of the steps, shelves were filled with potatoes that looked like the faces of old men, and rounds of pale cheese. On hooks overhead were dried sprigs of thyme and rosemary, and underneath, withered apples, the last of fall's harvest. I was almost drunk with their sweet smells.

Ours. All of it. Miller had said that once.

That fierce feeling grew inside me each day.

At night I no longer slept in the loft. Mother and I shared the bed near the hearth. I awoke dozens of times, listening to the tree frogs. They were sentinels. Should something disturb them, even a footfall, their music would stop.

Half-asleep, I thought of the river and the bateau, a flat-bottomed boat that had carried us here when I was four years old. Mother and Father had brought John across the ocean from the

Palatine before I was born, searching for freedom from the French swords just across the Rhine. In the new country, they'd worked on one farm after another until they were able to settle on their own land.

That day Father had stood in the front of the bateau, shattering the river's thin crust of ice with his pole. I'd leaned out to push against the skim of ice with my palm, watching black water appear that numbed my hands, until Mother pulled me back by my petticoat. "Zee, what will we ever do with you?"

Beside her now, I slept again.

∽

When trouble came, it wasn't night. There was a hint of daylight, and mist still floated above the fields. The tree frogs slept.

The chicken coop went first.

I walked between the house and the coop, swinging a pail of corn. There was a curl of smoke, a twist of gray, and before I had time to move, the roof exploded. Pieces of wood flew off, and in the opening, orange flames shot out.

The pail clattered away from me as I ran to open the door. The rope was gone, burned away, and I wasted moments trying to dig my nails into the rough edges of the door to free the poor hens.

Smoke came up from around the base of the coop, thick and black, and I stepped back, horrified by the pain of the hens. I took in great gulps of air until I heard Mother screaming, "Run, Zee! Go!"

The house was in flames. Mother was in the doorway and men were around her. In the dim light, I couldn't see who they were. I started toward her, coughing, retching, and she screamed, "Go!"

One of the men separated himself from her and moved toward me. I flew. Barefoot, breathless, I clambered over the rocks between the fields, trying to reach the safety of the trees. I remembered the rabbit and the hawk.

I was the rabbit.

His footsteps were light and sure; he knew the ground as well as I. A Loyalist from the valley, then, or one of the Indians. If I had turned, I might have seen who he was, but there was no time for that.

The trees came closer. They were thick and the ground was overgrown. I reached them, darting between them, backing up against a trunk with rough bark. Don't move, I told myself, don't cough.

I was Old Gerard's pupil, after all, and whoever was chasing me passed by. Had I reached out, I could have touched him.

I bent over, my hands on my knees, trying to catch my breath, to slow the beating of my heart. What should I do?

Gerard came to my mind. Gerard would tell me.

I waited until I saw glimpses of the sun directly overhead, and then I went toward his lean-to, not on the path I usually took, but along its side.

I didn't call out, but he heard me coming. As quiet as I was, I could never surprise him. He held out his arms, and I fell into them. "What have you done to your hands, child?"

I looked down. They were blackened, charred, but strangely, there was no feeling in them.

He motioned to Elam, who was in the doorway. Elam went for a cup of water, and Gerard held it, icy cold, to my lips. Nothing had ever tasted so fine.

But what about Mother?

My words tumbled out: the house, the coop, Mother. Gerard listened. And then we were both silent for a moment.

"She was right," he said. "You must go."

"I have to go back to her."

He shook his head. "Don't go back."

I didn't answer. I knew she was gone, that the house was gone, that there was nothing left to go back to.

I wanted to sink under Old Gerard's walnut tree and

close my eyes. If only I could wrap my arms around myself until the trembling died down, until I could stop thinking about the whoosh of fire as it had gone through the roof of the coop. If only I could forget the moment I'd seen the house, seen the black smoke coming from the doorway. But most of all, I wanted to stop seeing Mother with those dark shapes around her.

I couldn't stay; I knew that.

Gerard went into his lean-to and came out with a clay jar. He covered my hands with a thick poultice that smelled of bark, and grease, and maybe rum.

My hands felt as if they were encased in thick mitts, and my fingers were stiff. As he helped me lie down, I knew I had the beginning of a fever.

I slept for what must have been hours, and awoke at last to see Gerard coming across the field. Elam followed, head down, a spade in his hand.

I sat up. They had buried Mother. Mother, with her soft face, her warm hands. Gerard and I looked at each other in silence.

"Under the trees, I've marked her grave with a stone," he told me. "I think it is a good place for her."

"I'm grateful," I said, my voice strangled. Only that morning she had turned the cheese in its tray.

I saw then that the sun was a red ball beyond the fields. "I must go," I told him.

He nodded and I could see the pity in his dark eyes.

I almost asked him to come with me, almost blurted out the words I can't go alone. How do I know where to go? But I knew that as long as he was alive, he'd stay there, straddled between the Patriots and the Loyalists.

"You will go north," he said, "and somehow find your father and your brother." He held out a cloth bag he'd filled with more of the poultice, a water jug, dried meat, fire starters, and lengths of linen for my hands.

I thought of the piece of parchment I had carried with me since the day Father had left. It would show me the lines my feet had to travel, the high points I'd climb first, the earth gentling out, rolling in front of me, the sweep of the rivers I'd have to cross.

Gerard spoke again. "You will have to find your way. You won't know whether those you'll meet are friends or enemies. Stay alone; keep to yourself until you are sure."

I half listened to his reminder about what to do for thirst and hunger. I was thinking it would take weeks to find Father and John. I looked down at my hands. What use would they be?

The sun had disappeared, but the sky to the west was shot

through with its rays. "You must leave now," Gerard said, "before someone realizes you are here."

I stood, and he eased the bag over my shoulders. He slashed some of the linen into pieces with his knife and wrapped them gently around my hands. He touched my forehead, and then I turned, my eyes burning, and went toward the field. When I was halfway across, he came after me and dropped his knife into the bag.

How could I leave him?

Almost blind from tears, I stumbled away.

My head told me to go north, but my feet knew where I belonged, and that was the path I took. I skirted the trees until what was left of the house was in front of me: the blackened logs, the spirals of smoke still wafting upward, and the chimney standing high and alone. The land was scorched, the corn shriveled away. The stench of it burned my nostrils.

I waited, watching, until it was almost dark, and then I went closer. Nothing was left of the chicken coop but ashes. The cow was gone, and the sheep.

Oh, Father, your sheep, a Loyalist prize.

For the first time, I thought about Stout Lucy, our irritable cat. Did you escape, Lucy? Please be safe.

The house door hung there. How strange, a door that was supposed to protect us led to nowhere. I stood outside, seeing floorboards that were still smoking. The linens, and even the bed, had burned away. The pot on its hook in the hearth was covered in soot.

I wept, my hands held high in front of me. There was no strength in my fingers to open the cellar door. I was glad I wouldn't see what had happened to the herbs, the apples, and the potatoes that looked like old men's faces.

One of Mother's spoons and her iron kettle lay close to the doorway. I could see that spoon in her hand; I could see her grasp the kettle's handle, pouring water into a cup. I managed to slip the spoon into my bag and loop the kettle over my arm.

How foolish. Oh, Zee, what will we do with you?

Even more foolish, I curled up against the door outside, my head against the splintered wood, and slept.

My dreams were strange. Weird dark shapes wandered in and out of them, and a voice said, Hurry, Zee.

I awoke to a terrible thirst. I didn't try to unstop Gerard's water jug, but walked slowly to the river's edge.

I lay in the mud, drinking, the water cooling my mouth, my throat. I walked into the shallows; the cold water bathed my fever while above hundreds of fireflies blinked their yellow-green lights.

I thought of a hot July night the past summer. Who could have slept in that damp heat? Together Mother and I had tiptoed out the door and watched the fireflies. Mother's hand had been on my shoulder; I could almost feel it there now.

How could I live without Mother?

I thought of John; I thought of Julian and Miller, whose father had the gristmill down the road. Miller trying to make me laugh when I was in a testy mood. And then his face in front of me one night last summer: "Who doesn't fight for what belongs to him?"

And now I knew he was right.

If John had been here . . . If Julian and Miller had still lived just over the hill . . . And Father? If.

I had done nothing to save Mother, to save our house.

Fiercely, I promised myself: I would be different. I would be strong and tough. Never again would I let anyone take away what was mine.

I turned to look at the ruin behind me, a smoldering mass. It was the last of home. I went back to the doorway for the bag and began to walk.

TWENTY-FIRST CENTURY

It's Saturday night. Elizabeth sits opposite Libby at the kitchen table eating dinner: wrinkled peas and chicken tenders. The peas were cooked too long, the tenders not long enough.

It's late. They waited all afternoon at the arts and crafts shop, not willing to leave the drawing. They chose a narrow silver frame and bent over looking at the back of the drawing while the shop owner talked on the phone.

"Strange," Libby said as they stared at the pale markings: the three triangles, the center one towering over the other two, and the lines meandering across the page. What could those marks have possibly meant to Zee?

Elizabeth finishes the last of her dinner and looks across at Libby. "I'm going to change," she says. She feels almost desperate about it. "I'm going to save money and pay for the frame." She takes a breath. "I'm going to start my life over, be more careful."

Libby laughs. "Your mother was always starting over, too." She goes to the china closet and pulls a picture out from the bottom drawer. "I meant to give you this."

A seven- or eight-year-old girl smiles out at her from the photo. "You know that her name was Sarah," Libby says. "We called her Sisty."

She was real, Elizabeth's mother who died when Elizabeth was a baby. She wasn't an angel who floated around on a cloud somewhere, like the one in the Christmas card picture Elizabeth keeps in her dresser drawer.

"How much she loved you," Libby says.

Elizabeth's eyes burn. Strange, she's never once cried for her mother. She glances toward the hall. The drawing is back on the wall: Zee, another person who once was real. And Elizabeth's mother looks a little like Zee.

Libby clears her throat. "I've been thinking about my cousin Harry."

A name Elizabeth doesn't know.

"He's a second cousin, I guess," Libby says. "We used to spend holidays together when my grandparents were alive." She smiles. "Your great-grandparents."

Elizabeth thinks of holidays. Her mother would have had Thanksgiving dinner with great-grandparents Elizabeth has never heard of, and maybe Christmas with Harry, whoever he is.

"Harry would know much more of the family history," Libby says, and veers off to talk about Zee's fire. She ends with "It was neighbor against neighbor here during the Revolutionary War."

That one word intrigues Elizabeth.

Here.

Neighbor against neighbor here.

All this time, she's thought the Revolutionary War was far away. Maybe down on Long Island, or in South Jersey. "Here?"

"Zee's farm was north of Deposit, along the Delaware River," Libby says. "That was the frontier."

Elizabeth can't believe it. An hour or two by car, maybe.

"They burned her out," Libby says. "Was it Loyalists? Iroquois? No one knows. But they burned the farmhouse down, and the outbuilding. I walked that land when I was a child. Harry and I did that. He still lives there." She raises one shoulder. "There's nothing left, just the fields, the river, and Harry's house."

Elizabeth blows across the surface of her tea. Zee had a place. She lived in that place.

"It's strange about family stories," Libby says. "The first generation remembers all of it, but what passes on to the next is just in pieces, and those pieces get smaller and smaller. . . ."

This is a lot for Libby to say at once, Elizabeth thinks as she leans forward, waiting for more.

"After the fire," Libby says, "Zee went to find her father. We know that much. And we know about the cave. I remember my grandmother telling me the story. Zee's father was fighting somewhere in the north."

She leans forward, too. "Remember, her hands were

burned. There were no antibiotics, no medical help. She nearly died in that cave. Can you imagine? A young girl alone. Her mother gone—"

Libby breaks off. She must realize what she's saying.

But Elizabeth wants to hear it all. "Don't stop."

Libby smiles at her. "You can read the next part of the story in the library. Zee left things in the cave—"

Elizabeth puts her cup down without looking. It clatters onto the edge of the saucer and spills. She mops at it with her paper napkin. "Sorry."

Libby waves her hand. "Don't worry," she says, and goes on. "No one knows what was in the cave, what are still in the caves that riddle the mountains. People who cleared out left things they couldn't carry. But after the war, there were mudslides, and caves were buried. People looked for those caves for years. Harry looked."

Elizabeth nods. There's so much for her to think about. So much for her to take home and remember.

"We'll just have to go to Harry's. I know you'll want to talk to him," Libby says. "It's the last day before your father comes." She says this as if the words are being pulled out of her.

One last day for Elizabeth to know Zee, to take Zee with her. She'll hold on to the way Zee looks, her eyes, the silly cap, even the lines on the back of the drawing. She wants to remember all of it forever.

Libby grins at her. "We won't even call Harry to say we're coming. We won't give him the chance to say no." She wipes her face with her napkin. "Harry can be"—she hesitates—"difficult."

She shakes her head. "I was the shy one. I never opened my mouth, and Harry was mostly grumpy. It was your mother who kept us friends, kept us laughing. After Sisty died, we just stopped seeing each other. I always meant to get in touch with your father, to see you. The years got away from me."

Elizabeth takes a sip of her water, the ice cubes clinking.

"Harry knows more about Zee than I do," Libby says, "and at least you'll have that."

At least, Elizabeth thinks.

zee

EIGHTEENTH CENTURY

The path ran along the side of Big Fish Water like a ribbon. I followed it as the sun came up, a red-hot ball over the trees, a fire against the side of my face. My mouth felt like the dust at my feet.

How could I be so thirsty when I could see all that cool water rushing over the rocks and frogs, splayed out, their throats swollen with mating songs?

The night before, I had slipped into that water to drink, letting the thirst go downstream with small swirling sticks, and leaves, and fish the river carried. Had it been the night before?

I walked on. I knew I was ill and fevered and not thinking properly. And despite my thirst, it was too much effort to kneel down and put my face in the water.

Every step I took was an effort.

Suppose I left the bag Old Gerard had given me. It was heavy. Or I might let Mother's kettle go, but the clank of it with each step was comforting.

Something was wrong with my hands.

What had happened to them?

Ahead of me were the mountains. The tall one picked up glitter from the sun and almost glowed in its light. The other two, one on each side, leaned toward each other.

"See there, Ammy," I'd said once, pointing. "Sisters whispering to each other."

"Which one are you?" she'd asked. "Which one am I?"

"I'll be the tall one, the glittering one."

She'd touched my shoulder. "We will call that one Zee."

Now I crossed over the rocks, slippery with moss, to the other side of the river and began the climb upward.

The land rose gently, but still my breath was loud and uneven. Ahead of me, the sisters no longer had the look of green velvet we'd seen from the distance. Among the evergreens were silver boulders. Browning trees that had fallen the past winter were held up by their neighbors. Neighbors helping each other.

I was glad for the shade overhead. I pictured Mother reaching out, Mother's cool hands, and thought about making soap. My petticoat was stiff with mud. "Needing soap," I said aloud.

I hadn't made soap; I remembered that. And remembering the Patchins reminded me we'd come up this mountain the past summer. Isaac and Ammy, Miller and Julian, John. We were gathering . . .

Blueberries in the mountains?

"These are soft mountains," Miller had said, "worn from centuries of wind and water."

My cap had caught on a branch, and Isaac had loosened it, smiling down at me. How tall he had grown.

Something about that summer day . . .

There had been a cave, hadn't there?

Miller had warned me: "Be sure the cave is empty. It's a place for black bears, cubs and their mothers who would take a sweet bite of you."

I couldn't go farther. I began to count my steps. Seventy, seventy-one. Began again. One, two—

And there was the entrance to that cave.

Beyond the entrance, I saw movement.

Not Isaac. Not Julian or Miller. How fuzzy my thoughts were.

I remember Miller moving rocks that summer day until he had

made a circle of stones so we could sit. He'd given me the flattest one. We'd all eaten the blueberries, blue juice dripping.

Leaves on a low bush quivered. I stood still, watching. Squirrels flitted overhead. Mourning doves called in their sad voices.

The cave had been empty last year. That was as far back as I could think. I ducked my head and entered. It smelled of damp and maybe something dead. The ceiling was low and I could not stand straight.

I dropped Old Gerard's bag, and the kettle clattered away. I crouched down to sit against the rocks, to stare outside at the green world. I pulled the bag closer, remembering that my hands were burned, remembering the poultice.

Mother was gone. And I was alone.

I opened the bag and pulled off a bit of the dried meat, but it made me gag.

I unwound the cloths from my hands, the thick poultice sticking to the linen. My skin looked strange; some spots were blackened, others pink.

I slathered on more of the poultice and thought about wrapping the linens around my hands again.

Slept.

∽

When I awoke, it was dark, but I could see the pale path the moon made through the cave opening.

My forehead was burning, burning. My lips were thick, dry. I reached for the water jug and took a sip, watching water drip down my arm like a thin stream of rain running off a tree branch.

Stiff hands.

Slept.

∽

I awoke suddenly to another day.

How much time had gone by?

And I was alone.

I looked up at that rock ceiling. I'd never been alone before. Mother had been there, or Father. Ammy planting with me in the field. John. Isaac. Julian and Miller. I had dreamed about Miller. He'd helped Father the past winter, shoveling heavy snow from the roof, grinning down at me.

I picked up the water jug, which lay on its side. It had no weight to it: almost empty, then.

I pushed myself up against the wall with my feet and held my hands out in front of me, my fingers too stiff to bend. How would I ever get to Father? To John?

No one was there to tell me what to do. "Think," I told myself aloud. "Think by yourself."

I needed water. I needed to eat.

I looked around me in the dim light. The linens for my hands lay across the cave floor. I must have shaken everything out of the bag, because Mother's spoon was on the ground, too, and so was the map Father had drawn.

I pulled in my breath. The meat was gone. An animal had come close to me during the days I had been there. A small animal, I hoped. I shuddered, thinking about it.

Never mind. Water first.

I'd have to go down the mountain to the river.

It was so far, too far.

It had to be done. I inched my way out of the cave, holding the jug under one arm.

Outside, the sun's narrow rays filtered through the trees. I held my face up to the light, to the warmth. I was alive.

I heard the gurgle of water nearby and looked up. A thin stream splashed its way down the side of the mountain. I ran forward and knelt, my face in that water, gulping, drinking until I couldn't hold any more. I leaned forward. With both palms holding the jug, I managed to fill it.

How lovely it would be to stay there for a while, to soak up the sun, to listen to the water spilling over the rocks. But I had to use my time well.

I went back to the cave and took the filthy linens to the stream. I couldn't pound them, but I held the ends and let them drift in the water until they were the color of cream again.

I moved into the deepest part of the stream, hands raised, and let the water do its work. It leeched the mud out of my petticoats, and underneath, my feet and legs felt new and clean.

The rocks were slippery. I took a misstep, and my feet went out from under me. I slid gently into the water.

How cold it was, icy; my teeth began to chatter. Gently, I lowered my hands into that cold. I sat there until I was bathed to my neck, my clothes floating around me.

I would find Father. I would find John. And together we'd go back and take what was ours.

EIGHTEENTH CENTURY

That night stars crowded the sky. I stood outside the cave. Hunger gnawed at me. I would leave here as soon as it was daylight, and find food.

Last fall, I'd walked through the trees with Isaac. Last fall, when we were neighbors. We had eaten together at the Patchins' farm, sharing the partridge, the elk, the deer, our faces stained red from elderberry juice.

I clamped my teeth together, my stomach twisting. It's all right, I told myself. I'm all right. My fever was gone.

Everything was ready. My clothes were almost dry against my body. The poultice was thick on my hands, and the clean linen cloths were wrapped around them. The map was tucked inside my bodice, and so was Old Gerard's knife.

For one more night I'd sleep in this cave that had sheltered me, then I'd go forward.

There was a rustle in the trees that surrounded me.

I saw . . .

What did I see?

Just the outline, the glow of eyes in the darkness.

A sound I could never describe.

An animal moved out of the trees toward me, growling deep in its throat.

I reached down, groping for a branch, for a rock, for anything to drive it away. But I had forgotten my useless fingers. I felt nothing. There was only the sound of brittle leaves as I disturbed them.

The animal sank down, watching me. Waiting.

I thought of Miller's warning. Was this an animal coming to claim its cave?

I had the knife. But how would my fingers wrap themselves around it? And to use that knife meant the animal had to be so close I would feel its breath on me.

I glanced at the cave entrance. Would I be trapped in there? I took a step away from the animal, away from the cave. I took a second step, and a third, putting a tree between us, careful of my feet as I moved, my eyes fixed on the animal. If I slipped—

But I wouldn't slip. I was determined not to slip.

I kept moving away until the animal was blocked from my view. At last, I turned and ran, bare feet landing hard on twigs, sharp stones cutting the soles, blisters breaking. Still I didn't stop until I had reached the top of the mountain.

In the light of the moon, I was able to look down and see our valley: the Patchins' house, the willow trees along the river, and our own fields.

I turned. Ahead of me, the trees were too thick to see the valley on the other side. But I knew it was there, with its bands of angry Iroquois, and roving troops of British soldiers. I would never see the Indians until it was too late; they moved swiftly, silently, as I well knew. Hadn't Old Gerard taught me to do the same?

But the British regulars were different. I had heard they were arrogant, dressed in their red coats, cocked hats on their heads. And what about those who wore the green jackets? The Royal Greens, they were called. Afraid of no one, they marched along in their shiny boots, proud of themselves and glad to be seen. I would hear them coming long before they heard me.

I was wide awake now and the path downward stood out clearly, so I went on, moving quickly. The land leveled out before morning, and I stopped to suck the moisture out of the low-hanging leaves.

Late in the day I rested. I was dizzy without food and longed for my first sight of the river. I thought of bass, gleaming silver. I thought of pickerel. Even the eels Gerard and I had caught each spring would taste well smoked over a fire.

A fire.

I was almost a day away from the cave. It was too late to go back. And what had I left there? The fire sticks. The poultice. But worse, much worse, all that was left of Mother was gone. The small spoon, smooth from years of use, and the kettle. How could I have forgotten?

I drew myself up against a tree. Somehow I would fish, somehow I would manage to eat what I caught without a fire.

And one day, I promised myself, I'd go back to the cave and find what I'd left behind.

By noon I reached a river and saw a small cabin perched at the edge of the water. I kept to the shelter of the trees and watched, but no smoke came from the chimney, no hens wandered around the front, pecking at the earth.

Still I waited, hardly able to stand, I was so hungry. I remembered the rabbit escaping from the hawk that day, and thought of the meal he might have made.

I tried to flex my fingers in their linen wraps but they bent only the slightest bit. The skin had grown so itchy it seemed worse than pain. I took off the linen and scratched at my hands until they bled.

All the time I waited for someone to come outside, but I heard no voices. I went forward at last, up the worn path to the door. It swung open under my fingers.

When my eyes grew used to the dim moonlight, I saw food: strawberries in a bowl, early peas, blueberry preserves, a round of cheese on the table.

Food. I threw myself on it and ate.

TWENTY-FIRST CENTURY

Elizabeth works with Libby in the kitchen, packing a picnic lunch of sorts: slices of turkey on deli rolls, bakery cupcakes with swirls of chocolate icing, and a couple of bananas with dark spots on the peels.

Libby stands at the counter. She pats the sandwich bags and the cupcakes, wrapped in foil. "Ah," she says, and adds a six-pack of water.

"I think we should take the drawing with us," Elizabeth says, "and show it to Harry."

But Libby shakes her head. "Better we keep Zee here, where she belongs."

Elizabeth wanders into the hall and stares up at Zee's face. How did she ever think Zee wasn't pretty? No, *pretty* is the wrong word. There's something else going on there; whatever it is escapes her.

She runs her finger over the glass, following the strand of

hair that forms a line across Zee's cheek. She touches the wisps of Zee's eyebrows, the smudges on her kerchief.

Did the artist put those smudges in? Was she that much of a mess, or have the marks gotten there by themselves all these years?

And what about the artist?

Libby comes in from the kitchen, wiping her hands, and looks over Elizabeth's shoulder. "I wonder who drew this. There's love in every line."

Elizabeth looks up at Libby in surprise. She sees the same thing.

If only she'd shown the drawing to Mrs. Baxter, the art teacher at school, when she had the chance. Mrs. Baxter was talking about "seeing the artist through his work." It's a shock to understand what she meant. Mrs. Baxter might not be such a flake after all. "If you look carefully," she said, waving her paint-stained hands around, "you'll see more than you expected. It's the same with people." Everyone laughed, because she'd rubbed her cheek and left a smear of bright blue paint there, too.

At last Elizabeth and Libby are in the car, backing out of the driveway. It's almost eleven. What has happened to this morning? Elizabeth has to hold on to today. It has to last her forever.

Libby glances at her. "We'll take Route Seventeen north past Deposit. Of course, towns weren't there during the Revolutionary War, just small farms."

Elizabeth realizes suddenly that they've both been talking easily together lately, and even when they're silent, they're comfortable with each other.

Libby begins to tell her about her mother. "Sisty made up stories at night when the two of us were falling asleep." Libby turns to her. "I told you that we slept in the bedroom that's yours now."

Elizabeth pictures her mother tracing the outlines of the quilt houses with her fingers, imagining people who lived in the houses, as Elizabeth has been doing.

She leans her forehead against the window as the Catskill Mountains rise on each side of them. Everything is green, washed-looking, and sparkling streams flash by. A fisherman in waders stands knee-deep in the water, his line an arc over his head.

They stop in a rest area to eat, Elizabeth taking quick bites of her sandwich, hardly tasting what's in her mouth.

They drive on, the bright sun overhead. Elizabeth closes her eyes, dozing; music from the radio lulls her. She feels the car turning, the wheels scattering stones on gravel as they leave the highway. She sits up straight, rubbing the pins and needles out of one foot on the back of her other leg.

They're almost there, going through mountains that Zee must have seen, might have climbed. Elizabeth studies the narrow river that winds around; it's almost as if the river is leading them on. She glances up at those mountains glittering in the strong light.

They look as if they're talking to each other, commenting maybe on the sun warming their rocky bones.

Her mouth goes dry.

In front of them are three gentle peaks covered in green.

The tallest is in the center.

Three triangles.

Elizabeth can hardly breathe. A bird glides over one of the peaks, and she knows the feeling it must have. She feels as if she's flying now, as if she's gliding.

She keeps staring at those mountains. She knows what they mean; she knows those triangles.

How is it that she and Libby hadn't guessed what the lines meant?

On back of Zee's drawing is a map. And it begins here.

EIGHTEENTH CENTURY

I'd eaten too much, too quickly. I put my hands on the roundness of my waist, smoothed down the fullness of my skirt. All that food made me sleepy, and the pallet in front of the hearth was inviting. But first I looked at Father's map; I studied the lines, wondering how long it would take to work my way through them.

As I looked around that small house, I saw that the strawberries were fresh, their color a sharp red. They'd been picked today, or yesterday. Someone must live here; someone who might be back soon.

Suddenly I was wide awake. I scrambled out the door, closing it behind me, and ran for the trees. I didn't stop until I was well away from the house, glancing back over my shoulder, wishing I were faster, wishing I had not eaten so much. Looking backward instead of forward. Creating enough noise to alert every animal that might be nearby.

What would Old Gerard have said to me, raising one leathery finger after the other?

Do nothing without a plan.

Go silently.

Face your enemies.

None of that did I do. I crashed through the trees, stones sharp under my feet, roots waiting to trip me. I was out of breath, gasping—

And ran headlong into two men.

Behind them a group of five or six more came silently, slipping around the trees at my side.

Please. Let them be on my side. Let them be Patriots.

How strange that both Patriots and Loyalists looked the same, dressed the same, loved the land the way I did. How did I know, then, that this was the enemy?

I knew.

Old Gerard's voice was in my mind: Show strength, never weakness. But that I could not do. I stared at them, surrounding me now. I was terrified, my useless hands out in front of me.

"Who are you?" one of them asked. He wasn't young. His

face was as leathery as Old Gerard's, but his eyes were gray, pale and angry.

"I am Zee." My voice sounded strange. I hadn't used it since I'd left home.

"Spying." His eyes were hard now, like chips of stone.

I began to shake my head. But then I saw who stood toward the back of them. Isaac, with his sunburned face, the freckles scattered across his nose! And he saw me.

I drew in my breath.

How old had we been, Isaac and I? Ten? Splashing at the edge of Big Fish Water. "Don't move," he'd said. He was strong even then; he had both hands around my waist, swinging me out and above the water to escape a snake moving under us, a slow-moving wave.

I stared at him now. You could never forget me, Isaac. I am Zee. We are—

"She's a friend," Isaac said, coming to stand next to me. "A neighbor."

"Someday—" he had said.

He looked at me now with the smile I'd seen since the day Father had guided the boat ashore and built our house, the boy I had kissed that day in the river as he'd set me safely down away from the water moccasin. I had seen that smile only for me.

I saw the shock in his face. Was it because we were there in this forsaken woods? Or was it because of the state I was in?

He lifted his hand, and I could see he was wondering about my own. "She's going to safety in the north," he said. "Going to Canada, where it is easier to be loyal to the king."

"Alone?" What disbelief there was in the man's gruff voice!

"They are behind me, my family; they are coming," I said.

The man gave his head a quick shake, staring first at me, and then at Isaac. But finally he turned to the others. "We'll go back to the cabin to eat."

I heard the intake of my breath. What would they do to Isaac when they saw what I had done?

"I took cheese," I said. "I took fruit."

To my amazement, the man began to laugh. "Such honesty makes me think you must be one of us," he said, his eyes dancing.

Then they were gone without disturbing a leaf or a twig, gone silently. All except for Isaac.

"I will walk a way with you," he said.

He reached out to take my hand. But I couldn't let him do that. It was not only because of the pain it might cause, but because I knew how those hands would feel to him: coarse, the skin stretched and webbed. My nails were cracked; I was going to lose them.

I stepped away from him, but he put his hands on my arms, his face close to mine. "What happened, Zee?"

I could hardly speak, and when I did, my voice was bitter. "They killed Mother and burned the house."

"Who?"

I shook my head. "I couldn't see them clearly. Not English, though. Whoever it was knew the land. One of them followed me."

Isaac would come with me now. I wouldn't be alone.

He straightened my cap gently. "Did you not think to go to my parents?"

"They are gone to Canada. Ammy told me."

"Canada!" I heard the pain in his voice. "Canada!" He took a breath. "And so you are seeking your brother."

I nodded.

"I promise you this," he said, and there might have been tears in his eyes. "This fight will be over, perhaps even in a year, Zee. The king's men will win, of course. You know that. We will go back and rebuild your house, and someday—"

Someday—

Anger roared through me. "I have lost almost everything." I

held out my hands. "Do you think I will ever live under a king? I will fight with my father and my brother. Make no mistake, Isaac. We will win because we are desperate to win."

I didn't wait for him to answer. I brushed past him, then turned. "There is still the land. You will never take that from us."

EIGHTEENTH CENTURY

It was a long way north. The days ran into each other as I walked through the forest. And then weeks. There was no church meeting to prepare for on Sunday, no cheese pan to turn, no wash to hang on Monday.

But I knew the hours. I watched the trail of the sun as it beamed through the thick trees; its first sighting in the east would have been the moment to let the hens out, to throw the corn in golden arcs as they pecked at my feet.

With the sun straight over my head, warming my cap, it would have been time for cheese and a crust in front of the hearth, and sometimes on Sundays, a meal of one of the hens. Later I'd escape from the house to lean on the split rail fence and talk to Isaac.

I didn't want to think about Isaac.

I followed the wider river that Father had marked on the map, finding berries to fill my mouth. They never quite filled my stomach.

I slept after that. And sometimes when I awoke, in spite of myself, I thought of Isaac. I told myself I would never see him again, and that was the truth of it. After the war, if our side won, Isaac would follow the big mountains to the east, around the lakes to Canada. He'd spend his days near Mistress Patchin, with her quick tongue, with kind Mr. Patchin, and Ammy.

Oh, Ammy.

And oh, Isaac. He'd have another girl to swing up out of a river. He'd sit with another girl on a split rail fence.

So let there be another girl, a foolish girl who was willing to live under a king.

⁀

I was sorry to lose the sun as it set in the west, but I wasted no time in finding the best place to sleep. It had to be a spot where I could see everything, but not be seen; somewhere safe.

On that warm night with the sound of insects around me, buzzing and singing, so I felt less alone, I curled myself around a sugar maple tree, pulling my top petticoat up and under my head.

I lay there listening to the click of the crickets, the call of the tree frogs, the hoot of an owl.

I must be close to Fort Dayton now. The ground rolled just the slightest bit, but was much flatter than the land I had walked before this. How was I going to find it?

I pulled out my map, even though it was too dark to really see the lines. It was a comfort just to hold it in my ruined hands.

I fell asleep, reminding myself that I would reach the larger river soon, the Mohawk River. Until that happened, I wouldn't worry about finding Fort Dayton.

Morning came, a beam of sunlight in my eyes, and hours later I reached the river. I had expected a narrow band of water, one similar to the Big Fish Water at home. This was much wider.

A line of bateaux were passing close enough that I could see men on the decks. I counted four boats churning the water into foamy wakes; there might have been a fifth ahead of them.

I stayed behind the trees, watching, until the last one was opposite me. The deck was covered with cloth bags and a cannon, shiny black and ugly.

But whose boats were these? Were the men ours or were they Loyalists? I stayed in the shelter of the trees, not sure. If only I could call out to them. If only I could find out where Fort Dayton was.

As the last boat slid away, my chance to ask was fast disappearing.

I took a breath, picked up my petticoat, and slid down the bank. I paid no attention to my feet as they trod upon sharp stones at the river's edge. "Please," I called.

The men were facing away from me, staring down at the water's wake.

I waved my arms over my head. I shouted again.

One of them turned. He was close enough for me to see his fair hair under his hat. He leaned across the railing, staring at me curiously.

"Which way to Fort Dayton?" I called.

He raised his arm, pointing. "Find a boat and cross the river. Go north. You'll find Dayton." He cupped his hands around his mouth as the bateau slipped away. "We're on the way with supplies for Fort Stanwix. Going to shore it up against Colonel St. Leger."

I watched him until the bateau was only a small smudge on the river. St. Leger, I thought, remembering that name. He was an Irishman, a colonel in the British army, coming to help cut the colonies in two.

I felt a hint of fear. I was close to Father and John now, but also closer to the war itself.

I went to find a boat.

elizabeth

TWENTY-FIRST CENTURY

Elizabeth sees the house from the dirt road; it's red, with peeling paint, but a narrow band of river sparkles in front. "It's an old house," Libby says as she shuts off the car motor, "built in the early nineteen hundreds."

Elizabeth sees someone come out onto the porch. It must be Harry. He stares at them as they walk around the side of the house, threading their way through an uneven row of apple trees.

He's almost bald and thin as a toothpick; he can't quite hide his surprise at seeing them.

Libby shades her eyes with one cupped hand. "It's me, Harry, Libby." Her voice is so soft Elizabeth wonders if he can hear her. Her neck is one big red blotch.

Elizabeth realizes something. Libby really doesn't want to be here. Libby's doing this only for her.

She takes a step forward, but she sees that Harry isn't

asking them to come up onto the porch. He says a few words, but she doesn't catch any of them.

Head up, Libby doesn't wait for an invitation. She climbs the three steps and sits herself down in one of the wooden rockers lined up in front of the railing.

She fans herself with one hand. "Warm for a spring day, isn't it?"

Elizabeth takes a breath, then slides around Harry and sits, too. She listens to Libby talking in fits and starts, backing up, starting over.

Libby's trying to get to the point.

Just say what's on your mind, Pop would have said. Elizabeth almost smiles: How will she ever leave Libby?

The rocking chair squeaks as Elizabeth looks at the field in front of them. It leans down toward the river, and it's almost as if the sun is scattering diamonds across the surface of the water.

Zee walked here?

Planted in these fields?

Picked fruit from trees that have long since fallen to the earth?

And what about that fire?

Over her head a barn swallow swoops in under the eaves. It's building a mud nest up there. How does the swallow get it all together? Elizabeth wonders. Why doesn't the mud dry up between the trips the bird makes back and forth?

"Do you like birds?" Harry asks around his pipe, interrupting Libby midsentence.

Elizabeth nods.

"Nothing better to do, the two of you, than come all the way up here?" he asks.

Elizabeth almost gets up off the rocker and goes back to the car. But in the distance . . .

In the distance are those mountains, wreathed in mist. She sees the three peaks from where she sits. Zee's mountains. It's amazing to know what something means, something that maybe no one else in the world does.

Zee must have seen those mountains from here. Did she look up at them the way Elizabeth does now? In spite of herself, Elizabeth makes a sound, raises her hand.

Harry turns again to stare. "What did you say?"

She stares back. "Just clearing my throat."

Libby begins again. "Elizabeth is interested in history. She thought—I thought—you might tell us about our family who lived here."

"I taught history for thirty-five years," he says. "If you think I want to teach it anymore, you've lost your mind."

Libby rocks gently. "I have a drawing of Zee."

Harry sits entirely still, the bowl of his pipe in his hand.

In that stillness, Elizabeth looks from one to the other. They know each other better than she thought. And something else. Libby is sure he's as interested in Zee as they are. He doesn't say, Who's Zee? He doesn't say, I couldn't care less about her. It's clear that he's trying to hide the excitement in his voice. "You never told me there was a drawing."

He wants to see that drawing, Elizabeth tells herself. He's dying to see it.

"Don't you know a little family history?" Libby asks.

"Can't remember much," he says.

And then, amazingly, Elizabeth realizes they're both trying to keep themselves from grinning.

Elizabeth rocks once, twice. "There's a map on the back of the drawing."

Both of them swivel around to look at her.

"A map to where?" he asks. Then he's talking to himself. "Could it possibly have been to Fort Dayton, or maybe Fort Stanwix? Someone in the family said once—" He looks off into the distance. "Zee was caught in the battle up there. If only I'd listened."

Elizabeth doesn't say a word. She's rocking with her eyes half closed, but she's memorizing: Fort Dayton, Fort Stanwix, names she's never heard.

"All right," Harry says. "Let's walk around." He stamps down the steps, not waiting to see if they follow.

Libby gives Elizabeth a little push. "I've done my part," she whispers. "And I know what he's going to show you."

When Elizabeth catches up, Harry points to the river. "They would have come up here to settle by boat," he says. "It was the only way to move a household. The trails would have been too tough, the forests almost impenetrable." He turns toward her. "What's your name, anyway?"

"Melissa," she says, testing him.

"Don't act like an idiot," he says. "It's—"

"Francesca."

He snorts. "They'd have chopped down the trees to clear the land, built a cabin with some of the wood, one room maybe, with a ladder to the loft."

They walk around the back of his house. "I've read books

about this area's history," he says. "One had details about the Loyalists setting fire to some of the houses. Zee's was one of them, burned to the ground. Her mother was killed."

He bends over. "Now look at this." He claws into the earth with his fingers and comes up with a crumbling bit of cement, or mortar, or dried mud.

"I dug for this all over the property," he says. "The chimney was covered with dirt and grass as if it had never been there."

Elizabeth sinks down and spreads her hands over the earth, patting the bits and pieces. "The chimney," she whispers. "All these years, and we're touching a piece of Zee's chimney?"

"Maybe."

"It kept her warm in the winter," she says, almost as if she's dreaming it. "If she walked down to the river, she'd look back and see the smoke. She'd smell the bread baking, or meat cooking."

They look at each other, both delighted. "Thank you," she says. "Thank you."

He grins, a different Harry. A Harry she's going to get to know.

He leans back on his heels. "There's a story about people hiding things in caves. Patriots fleeing from the Loyalists. Zee may have done that." He shrugs. "People searched for years, back and forth over this trail, over that one. It's ridiculous to even look anymore."

He turns to Elizabeth. Deep lines radiate from his faded eyes. "I looked myself when I was young."

"Who knows?" she says. "Maybe we'll find something."

He shakes his head. "I don't think so. But we might find what happened to Zee. That's really what we want to know, isn't it?"

We.

"Yes," she says.

She and Harry will follow the map. They'll see exactly where Zee went. She draws three triangles in the air with one finger. She points to the mountains. "The map begins there."

"Ah," he says, staring at them. "And summer's coming."

It's almost an invitation.

No, not almost.

It is an invitation.

And then she realizes. She won't be here. She'll be gone.

She walks down to the river and scoops up a small stone, thinking Zee might have done something like this.

She holds it in her hand, feeling its smoothness, picturing the stone breaking off from some ancient mountain and rolling over and over, and now it will stay with her.

EIGHTEENTH CENTURY

Finding a boat was easy. It wasn't a good boat, to be sure. The sides were filled with small holes, and stagnant water sloshed on the bottom. It would take on water quickly, and I was sure that whoever owned it had abandoned it long before.

With my clumsy fingers, it took long minutes to untie the knots in the rope that held it to a willow tree. And how could I use the oars with hands that were stiff and straight?

But somehow it had to be done, and the trip would not be long. I could see the opposite shore from where I stood. It was a clear day, without wind, and the river was flat. Even if the water in the boat rose to my waist, I could do it. I'd come this far.

I made the crossing early in the morning. I went in circles, one oar pulling harder than the other; then, as the hand on that oar quickly tired, the other oar pulled the boat in the opposite direction. But at last the boat bumped against the shore, and I was there, north of the river. I gave the boat a gentle shove and watched it rock its way downriver.

From behind me came the rattling of wagon wheels; I heard horses' hooves and the crack of a whip. I turned, ready to run, to hide.

A woman urged on the horse, her cap askew, and in back of her were three children. She pulled the wagon up next to me. "What are you doing here alone? Why aren't you at the fort?" Her eyes were wild, terrified. "Get into the wagon, child. I'll take you. But hurry. We must get to shelter before the British come."

I lifted my petticoat and climbed up over the wheel and onto the seat next to her. Before I could say a word, she used the whip, and we lurched down the rutted road.

"Fort Dayton?" I called over the noise.

She nodded, her mouth trembling. "We're expecting General Burgoyne with the British soon, coming down from Canada to the east. Joseph Brant, the Iroquois leader, is somewhere to the west. And Colonel St. Leger is on his way to surround Fort Stanwix. He wants to starve out the Patriots."

I listened to the rough wheels drumming against the earth.

I wasn't as frightened as this woman. Her hands were unsteady on the reins, her face flushed. I'd lost Mother, and our home. Everything was gone. All I wanted was to see Father, to see John. I shut out the thoughts of Isaac.

But what I had to tell them was the worst possible news. I thought of Mother, always busy, always working, always calm. I looked down at my hands and had a sudden picture of her hands. They hovered over an orphan kitten, holding a wet towel that dripped milk into its open mouth. "She'll live," Mother had said. "She's stouthearted." And Father's face, usually stern, had softened. I'd known it wasn't the kitten's small face that had caused his smile; it was his love for Mother.

Now the wagon veered away from the river, following a creek, and the road was worse. Branches overhead snapped against us. The woman lashed the horse, her body bent forward as if willing us to reach shelter. In back of me, a child was wailing, but she paid him no heed.

I turned, my hand out to comfort him, but the sight of my fingers frightened him more.

At last the woman gestured with her whip. In the distance was the fort. She took a breath, calmer now. The horse slowed down, foam along its poor mouth.

My heart began to race as I thought of those dear faces,

Father's and John's. I glanced at my hands again. I could use them better now, but if only they didn't have to see them. Looking down at my feet, I wished, too, that I had washed myself in the river.

The woman called out, and the gates swung open. She laid the whip over the horse's back, but gently this time, and the horse took tired steps past the guard.

Inside, all was confusion. Women sat on the ground, babies in their arms. Others were coming out of a church. And men, their footsteps hurried, went back and forth from one area to another.

I remembered to thank the woman as I let myself down from the wagon. But she barely glanced at me. "I don't know if we're safe even here," she mumbled.

I searched, looking into every male face, hurrying myself into and out of the church, staring into doorways, stopping myself from calling out. Who could hear me in this din of babies crying, men calling, someone singing in a language I'd never heard before?

I followed along the side of a rough wooden wall. I was safer than I'd been for days, for weeks. I felt the sun, hot even this late in the afternoon, and for the first time I cried.

I cried for Mother; I cried for Isaac and Ammy. I even cried for Mistress Patchin and her kind husband. I raised my hands to my face, feeling the webbing of the skin. So I cried for my hands, for the hens, for the henhouse, and for the house. I cried for Stout Lucy.

From behind, arms came around me. "Ah, Zee," the voice whispered.

elizabeth

TWENTY-FIRST CENTURY

"How did this happen?" Libby grips the steering wheel. "What will we ever do with him?"

Elizabeth turns to look over her shoulder. A filthy blue pickup truck follows them. That's Harry at the wheel.

"The house is a mess," Libby says. "Things piled on the bed in the downstairs guest room—" She breaks off, and Elizabeth realizes that she's the one who has made the mess. No, that's not it entirely. Libby's gotten sloppier since that first week, too.

"There isn't a thing in the refrigerator worth eating," Libby goes on.

Elizabeth reaches out and touches Libby's smooth hand on the wheel. "He won't care."

Libby raises one hand to her throat. "He knows I'm a terrible cook. He told me that once."

Elizabeth glances at her. "Harry looks as if he hasn't had a decent meal in his whole life."

In Libby's driveway, Harry lopes toward them from his pickup truck. He thrusts a faded book into Elizabeth's hands. "You may want to look at this," he says, then follows them into the hall to see the drawing. He stands there, hands clasped behind his back, leaning forward. "Oh, Zee," he says, and takes the picture off the wall.

"What are you doing?" Libby asks.

Harry looks over his glasses. "I won't hurt it, Libby. You know I won't."

Libby just shakes her head a little, so Elizabeth goes into the kitchen to find something to pry the frame away so she can show him the map.

Harry walks into the dining room with the picture and begins to work on the tiny nails in the back of the frame. "Forty years I've been searching for Zee. And all this time she's been hiding in Libby's hall." He glances at Elizabeth. "What a family resemblance. Amazing."

Elizabeth feels it to her bones. There's a line that stretches back for two hundred years; it connects her to Zee. To Libby. To this grouchy Harry. To her mother.

She belongs here. How will she ever leave? How can she? She tries not to think of Pop's face. "Excuse me," she says, and runs up the stairs and into her bedroom. She closes the door and leans against it, taking deep breaths. A moment later, Libby's at the door, whispering, "Elizabeth."

"I'll be right down." Elizabeth tries to sound normal, as if she's not drowning in tears.

"Let me in," Libby says.

116

Elizabeth moves away from the door. Libby takes a step inside and puts her long skinny arms around her. "I know," Libby says. "I feel the same way."

They stand there for a few minutes longer, and then Libby says, "We forgot Harry." She smiles a little. "And I have to do something about dinner."

Downstairs, Elizabeth watches as Harry takes the picture from the frame and turns it over. "Look at this, Elizabeth." His fingers hover over the mountains, over the circling lines. He looks up at her. "Would you go out to the truck? Somewhere there's a map we can write on."

In the truck, she goes through a mess of books, a half roll of Life Savers that might have been there for years, and a few pennies. Finally she finds a creased map in the glove compartment.

They spread Harry's map out on the table, and he traces Zee's route with a pen. "Do you see it, Elizabeth? Do you see it?"

The three mountains, Zee's mountains.

He shows her the Delaware River, the Catskills. "There's the Susquehanna," he says, "running to the Mohawk River." He stops; the pen circles. "And on the other side of the Mohawk is Fort Dayton."

"I don't see—"

"The fort's not there anymore, but that's where her map says she was going. Clear as day." He looks up. "Oh, yes, Dayton." His finger travels from there along the Mohawk River. "Here's Oriskany. I think she was there."

Elizabeth shakes her head, and he sighs. "You haven't heard of it? Everyone should know it, one of the bloodiest battles of the Revolution. They went from Fort Dayton, hoping to save Fort Stanwix."

Elizabeth smells the roast that's cooking in the kitchen. Libby cooks beef until it's leather. It'll take forever to get dinner ready.

And then Libby calls, "Elizabeth, would you mind setting the table?"

"Elizabeth can't set the table," Harry calls. "She's busy."

Libby laughs from the kitchen. "Sorry," she calls.

Harry says, "St. Leger came from Canada with his British soldiers. He picked up Loyalists along the way, and the Iroquois, all of them determined to take Fort Stanwix."

Where is Zee? That's what Elizabeth wants to know.

But Harry goes on. "Our side was a patchwork. The American army was mostly a bunch of farmers. The Oneidas were on our side, but the other tribes were with the British. It was a miracle that we won in the end."

He's back to the map again. "Our General Herkimer takes eight hundred men from Dayton. They walk along the Mohawk River toward Stanwix. But they don't know they're heading for tragedy. They don't know that Brant and his Iroquois are waiting to ambush them at the ravine in Oriskany." He closes his eyes. "The ravine is a deep hollow gorged out by water with only a narrow road through it. It's there that they're surrounded."

Elizabeth shivers.

"I'll take you to see it. More than half of them were slaughtered before they even realized they were surrounded. Tomahawked. Scalped. Bayoneted. Horrible. Imagine the pain, the blood. . . . The first time I saw the ravine, I cried.

A grown man, a tough grown man." He spreads his hands. "What determination they had to build this country."

Elizabeth's throat is dry.

But Libby stands in the doorway. "Dinner is ready." The dining room table is covered with the map, the frame, the drawing. "We'll eat in the kitchen," she says.

Harry smiles at Libby. He looks happy. And he's polite during dinner. He praises the roast, which is almost raw. Across from Elizabeth, he chews thoughtfully. Then his fork clatters onto his plate. He pushes back his chair. "I just realized . . ." He drops his napkin onto the table and goes back into the dining room.

Elizabeth follows, and they look at the drawing together.

"The mark in the corner here?" he says. "I've seen it before."

"Where?" She stares down at it. It looks like a couple of sticks tied in the middle.

"I can't remember." He shrugs. "But don't worry, Elizabeth, I'll try. I promise you that. And tomorrow we'll go up to Oriskany. I'll show you where it all happened." He waves his hand.

"I won't be here," she says slowly, feeling as if she's going to choke.

"Her father is coming to get her tomorrow," Libby says.

"Of course she isn't going home tomorrow. Call her father and tell him. Ridiculous. She's going to Oriskany."

Elizabeth looks at Libby. Is it possible?

It's as if Harry has read her mind. "Yes," he says. "Oriskany. Nothing will stop us."

Elizabeth and Libby look at each other and smile.

"Why not?" Libby says.

"Why not?" Elizabeth wants to hug them both.

When Pop calls, she asks him about going to Oriskany. He says yes right away. But there's something in his voice. She knows what it is. It's disappointment. He misses her.

She falls asleep reading Harry's book on the American Revolution. And she thinks about sitting with Pop at their kitchen table and telling him about all this, telling him everything.

EIGHTEENTH CENTURY

I couldn't stop crying, couldn't open my eyes. His arm circled my neck, and his broad hand cupped my shoulder.

In that terrible heat of August, it was hard to breathe. We were surrounded by the smells of horses and cooking and meat that had long passed its freshness. And the noise! People shouting to each other, their heavy footsteps going past; hens clucked, pigs grunted, cattle lowed.

But all of it seemed distant, unimportant, as I buried my head in his chest. How good it was to be able to cry. How good it was to be safe!

I knew I had to tell him about Mother and the house. "I must tell you—" I said, my voice thick.

"Shhh," he told me. "Shhh."

It was the most comforting sound I had ever heard. I thought about a summer long before. John and I had hid in the cornstalks, our hands over our mouths to stop our laughing. And Father, pretending to be a bear, had thrashed around inches away from us.

He picked up my hand now and ran his fingers over my scarred skin. "Oh, Zee."

This was not Father. Or John. My eyes flew open. "Miller!"

He stood. "Yes, of course."

Angrily, I brushed the tears from my cheeks. "Why didn't you tell me? How dare you—"

"How could you not know it was me?" He smiled, his teeth even. "But here you are, Miss Zee. Back to your ordinary self."

"Go away." I shook my poor hands at him. And then I realized I needed his help.

"Where are Father and John?" I asked. Dozens of people moved around us—no, hundreds. Faces I had never seen. Most of them were John's age, but there were old people, too. Men with grizzled hair and beards, women whose faces were lined and gray. Some were soldiers; some, like the woman I'd come with, were there for protection against the Loyalists.

And Julian, Miller's brother—where was he?

122

I must have spoken aloud. Miller's face was grim. "He's on a bateau somewhere along the river, bringing supplies to Fort Stanwix. We can only hope they get there."

"I saw boats," I said. Julian might have passed that close to me.

Miller reached for my hands. "What happened to you? How are you in this condition?"

Condition. He must have meant my filthy cap, my torn and stained petticoat. That anyone should see me this way!

I bit my lip. "My condition is no affair of yours."

"A moment ago I was not in such trouble with you." He put his hand on my arm. "Come. We'll find them."

I shook off his hand and followed without a word. We circled around people sitting, standing in knots talking, and children chasing each other.

Miller pointed out a squat man, built like a rain barrel, who nodded at me seriously. As we moved around him, Miller whispered, "That's General Herkimer, who will lead us into battle. We're longing to fight."

Of course. Miller and Julian had been fighting from the time they could stand on their feet, rolling on the ground, their clothes gathering up twigs and mud. But they were always laughing, and this was no laughing fight.

The British were my enemies, too. I tried to brush thoughts of Ammy and Isaac from my mind. Stubbornly, they stayed, but my tears were done.

We reached a group of men training in the center of the fort. At last! Father and John. John broke from the ranks to run to me, and Father looked up and followed.

A few yards away they hesitated, staring at me as if they were seeing a ghost.

Miller gave me a small push with one finger.

I turned angrily and then forgot him. It was Mother I thought of. Mother, her cheeks flushed, pulling the bread from its place over the fire, its crust shiny. It was the house on the river, the loft where I slept, and Stout Lucy.

All lost.

Without thinking, I held out my hands to see the shock on their faces. "Mother is gone, then," Father said, his words strangled.

"The house was burning," I said. "I saw her in front, surrounded by men." I raised my shoulders. "She told me to go, to run. Later Old Gerard buried her."

John reached out for my hands, his mouth unsteady, and Father's face was more stern than I had ever seen it. "My dear wife," he said. "And the house she loved is gone, too." He put his large hand on my shoulder. "You came all this way alone? Is that possible?"

I nodded.

"Such a long trip," Father said, and I saw the tightness in his jaw, the look in his eyes. Tears held back? "A hard trip even for a grown man." He pulled me to him.

Later I ate roasted corn and meat broiled on a stick until I couldn't hold any more, and then I slept through the rest of that day and part of the next.

I awoke to the sound of people running and men shouting. General Herkimer stood in the center of the parade ground, and around him all was confusion. "At last!" Miller said as he ran past me.

Father and John joined the crowd around the general as he announced that finally the Americans were to make the forty-mile march to Stanwix, where St. Leger had surrounded the fort.

Father held me to him, then John. And Miller stepped forward, to put his hand on my shoulder. "Be safe," he said. I saw that he was going to say something more, but he just shook his head.

Then they were gone.

But what of me?

Was I now to lose them again?

How could I let that happen?

No. I would go with them.

But shoes!

My feet were strong now, toughened by the rocks and branches and hard dirt they had trod over all these weeks. But still, if I ever hoped to match the pace of a marching army, I had to cover my feet. So I stole.

I darted one way and then another, searching. Who would be foolish enough to leave a pair of shoes unattended? Shoes that might work their way onto my feet. It was almost laughable to think about. But that was exactly what happened. Beside the church steps was a pair of shoes, a little large, but they would do. I scooped them up, promising myself that I'd bring them back when we returned.

I watched the endless lines leaving the fort, and waited. I had to stay far behind Father and John, at least until they could no longer send me back.

How angry they'd be when they learned I was following them into battle. But their anger could not match the grief I'd feel if I were to lose them a second time.

They were all I had left.

What came into my mind then was the ruin of our house.

I remembered the fireflies dancing above me as I'd stood in the river. What had I promised myself that terrible night? I would be as strong as John and Father. I would never let anyone take away what was mine.

I felt a ripple of that strength go through me. I was tough from all those weeks. I darted outside the massive gates of the fort behind a ragged group.

Men and boys were coming to join this march, hurrying along the road with weapons slung over their shoulders. Ahead of me the column stretched forward.

I stopped, bending to put on the shoes, listening to the sounds of an army. "We begin on Monday, four days into August," someone said. "We will long remember it."

By now the line must have stretched a mile, or maybe two, in front of me. In back, men wheeled supplies and provisions on great oxcarts, all to help those who would be holding Fort Stanwix against the enemy siege.

The carts were slow; their weapons were cumbersome. I found my place behind them. Alone, but not alone. Somewhere in those hundreds of men were Father and John, and even Miller.

We followed the north side of the river. The path was clearly marked from long years of travel, beaten down first by the

Indians and then by the settlers as they built lean-tos and cabins nearby.

Overhead the willows bent their slim branches toward us and offered shade. The birds were silent, terrified by our noise, or perhaps in awe of what we were about to do: save Fort Stanwix from Colonel St. Leger and his men.

zee

EIGHTEENTH CENTURY

We marched for long hours; by midafternoon, I fell behind, listening to the giant wheels of the oxcarts, and sank down to work my way out of the shoes. My skin had rubbed against the stiff material, raising blisters that broke and bled as the shoes were pulled away.

The march was slower now; only narrow trails were marked. How lucky I was that those carts lumbered through the trees at such a slow pace. I could keep them in sight but had time to dip my feet into the cool river water. Finally I left the shoes at the edge of the trail. Would I ever come back this way for them?

I hobbled along until two men leading the last cart heard me. They turned quickly, wondering, I supposed, if the enemy had somehow appeared behind them.

I spun around, too. Nothing was there but endless trees and a path of shattered branches and torn leaves.

I looked up at the men leading the cart, probably father and son. The young one smiled, his gray eyes crinkling; the other nodded.

I ducked my head. I knew how I looked, a filthy waif. My cap had been lost somewhere; my hair, knotted with burrs, hung loose to my waist. My petticoat was stiffened with mud, and shreds of the hem trailed on the ground.

The older man patted the side of the cart and swung me up onto the seat in front with them. We were quiet then. I listened to someone whistling a song on a cart in front of us. But the song broke off suddenly, and I thought about what terrible things might lie ahead.

I spent the first night under the wagon with them.

I should have felt safe there, but the voices of men crying out in their sleep made me tremble. They were afraid. As was I. My terror grew with each rustle of a leaf. What would it be like to be shot at with muskets? I raised my hand to my head. How terrible if an Iroquois warrior pulled up my hair and sliced off my scalp.

My lips quivered against my teeth, but I made myself think of Old Gerard, who had taught me: Be quiet in the face of danger. Be calm and still.

Finally I slept.

The next morning we followed the marchers as they forded the river to the south. "Better to cross here," the father explained, "than nearer the fort, where St. Leger will be ready to pounce."

The woods were almost impenetrable. For hundreds of years massive trees had crowded each other to reach for the sky. Only the slimmest path wound its way under them to show that humans had been there. It was barely fit for men, and certainly not for oxcarts. All day the forest rang with the sound of axes chopping at branches so we could get through.

At the end of the day, eight hundred men rested along a stretch that must have been two miles long. Glints of the sun still shone like burning coins on the forest floor. Mosquitoes buzzed, and smoke from cook fires made it hard to breathe. I slid over the side of the wagon, thanked the men, and began to search for Father and John.

An impossible task? It should have been. I searched among men along the path, tripping over feet, branches pulling at me, and suddenly there was Miller coming toward me.

Miller!

I almost said, Go away, you're always underfoot, but I closed my mouth over the words. The truth was that I was glad to see him, so glad.

He nodded as if he knew what I was thinking. I glanced up at his peeling, sunburned face, his clear blue eyes, and it came to me with sudden sharp pain: he might not survive the battle.

Would any of us?

His face was more serious than I had ever seen it. "What are you doing here, Zee?"

What was in those eyes? Was it fear? Fear for me?

"You must leave before the morning light," he said. "Find your way along the trail we've left. Go back."

Go back alone? Go back at all?

"It's too late for that," I said. "And you are not my father to tell me what to do."

"Who would want to be your father?" He smiled a little. "Disagreeable girl that you are." His hand went to my face, waving away a cloud of mosquitoes.

I stepped away from that hand. "Isaac would never speak so," I said.

"Isaac the traitor," he said bitterly.

We stood glaring at each other. Then he grasped my arm and pulled me forward. I stumbled along behind him and saw Father and John leaning against the trunk of an ancient oak.

They started up when they saw me. "How is it possible you are here, Zee?" Father said. He was angry; I could see that. "You never think."

He looked at John, almost desperately, I thought. "She has to go back," Father said. "But who is there to take her?"

I might have reminded him that I had come through the mountains, across rivers, and into the Mohawk Valley completely alone. But this was Father, not Miller, and I could not speak that way to him.

"She will have to go by herself," John said, and put his hand on my shoulder to soften his words.

Miller's eyes were on me, and I glanced up at him. "I've given it some thought," he said slowly.

"Do I need you to think for me, Miller?" I said sharply.

"She will not go back," Miller said. "I knew that from the start. How strong she's always been."

Strong? I glanced at him again quickly, surprised, pleased. He smiled, looking down at me. "Headstrong, then."

They stood in a circle around me, wondering what to do with me. But I was no longer the girl who had left the door to the henhouse open. I was no longer only the girl who had spilled the soap fat, who had burned the bread. I was another person entirely.

I would go to battle with them.

"There is still a half day's march. If she stays with the wagons," Miller said, "the pace will be easier."

That was true. I knew it would be hard to keep up with that marching army, even though we must be close to our destination.

"She will be safer in the rear, too," Miller told Father, as if I couldn't hear, as if I were just a child.

I didn't listen to the rest. I was so tired. Too tired to eat. Almost too tired to sleep. I went through the trees, not far from where they stood, and lay on the rock-hard dirt, looking at the motionless leaves above me.

It was much later when Father knelt beside me with water and a crust that I was hardly able to chew.

Father spoke. "I can only imagine what these weeks have been like for you, Zee. But I know you survived terrible things."

I felt a sudden burning in my throat. To have him say that was almost worth those weeks alone.

"The anger I feel is only because I want you safe. You and John are all I have now." His voice was thick. "And that small bit of land on the edge of the river."

"If I had stayed back," I said, "and something happened to you, I would have nothing."

He was silent, but even in the dimness, I saw that he understood. I reached up and put my arms around him. I had never done that in my life. I didn't have the courage to say that I loved him, but he knew that; I was sure he did.

I slept then until light sharpened the world around us, and we were faced with a day that promised to be hot. A terrible day ahead of us.

I ripped off a shred of my under petticoat to dip into a water jug and clean my face, then tied up my heavy hair so it would be out of my way.

Miller was in front of me. "I have a ride for you with men bringing up food supplies," he said. "There's only a small bit of room, but they promised it for you."

It was hard to thank him, but I did, telling myself I was truly grateful.

Father put his hand on my shoulder. "Remember what Old Gerard has taught you," he said. "Should it be necessary, melt into the trees, go back. Live, Zee. Live."

elizabeth

TWENTY-FIRST CENTURY

Elizabeth is up early, and Libby, too. "I still have to go to work today," Libby says. "Terrible, your last day, but—" She runs her hand over Elizabeth's hair. "You'll have an adventure."

"I'll tell you all about it tonight, every single thing," Elizabeth says as she and Harry get ready to leave.

It's a poor day for a Monday in spring, a morning filled with unrelenting rain. Moments later they're in the truck with rivulets of water running along the side of the road. Even though the windshield wipers beat back and forth, it's almost impossible to see.

Harry leans forward and swipes the pane. "The park will be closed," he says, sounding irritable.

Elizabeth wonders why they aren't turning back. But suppose they do. She pictures the day going forward: saying goodbye to Harry, going into the empty house to wait for

Libby, sitting in that chair for the last time, watching the rain cascade off the leaves, her full duffel bags behind her in the corner.

But Harry doesn't turn back. He's talking about Brant, the leader of the Iroquois.

Elizabeth had seen a picture of him in Harry's book and thought how cool he looked, slim and dark-eyed.

"His tribal name was Thayendanegea. A mouthful, isn't it? He was there with St. Leger." Harry glances at her. "The Iroquois wanted the British to win because the Americans were crowding them out, building farms smack in the middle of their hunting grounds, and pushing into their villages." He takes a breath. "Let's eat now. We're almost there."

She sits back, chewing on the sandwich Harry had made for her in Libby's kitchen. It was pretty bad, crusts off, edges ragged, and the cheese inside a poisonous yellow. He made one for Libby's lunch, too. It was worse than anything Libby could have ever put together.

At last they pull off onto the side of the road, and Harry is right. The park is closed, a thick chain looped low across the wide path. Who in his right mind would walk around this place today?

Harry drums his fingers against the steering wheel. He grumbles at the weather, at the closed battlefield site.

"Do you have an umbrella or something?" he asks.

Of course she forgot to bring an umbrella. But as they sit there, the rain tapers off. Shreds of mist rise in pale tendrils over the park grounds.

"That's more like it," Harry says, and opens the truck door. They step over the chain to stand on the grass, which squishes under their feet. She looks around, thinking, August, a summer day, hot, steamy, maybe; hard to move, Patriots wishing they could sink down, rest their feet, wipe their damp faces.

She must have said it aloud. Harry nods. He waves his hand over the expanse of lawn. "Mammoth trees crowded together, their branches laced into each other. The mosquitoes unrelenting. You couldn't see two feet into the woods on each side. There were some horses and carts, but most of them walked, carrying heavy muskets."

Harry stops, and she sees the park, its trees dotting the mown grass. "Coming from the fort are Brant's Iroquois, St. Leger's Englishmen, the Loyalists. Almost every family in the Mohawk Valley had men fighting on one side or the other, and many had brothers fighting on opposite sides."

They begin to walk, Elizabeth telling herself that Zee might have been right here; her own footsteps might cover Zee's.

Harry holds her elbow and pulls her back. She looks down into a narrow gorge, the bottom choked with trees and weeds.

Where did it come from? It was as if a giant had scooped out the earth, leaving the sides impossibly steep.

"The ravine," Harry says. "There was a narrow road made of logs. They started down strung out in a thin line all the way back." He shakes his head. "They crossed the stream on the bottom and started up. The enemy was hidden on both sides."

He doesn't have to tell her the rest. She sees how it was. The screams, the shouts, the noise as the enemy came out of the trees, howling, firing, shooting arrows, surrounding them.

Surrounding Zee.

How terrifying it must have been. Her fist goes to her mouth. "How many died?"

"Half," he says. "More than four hundred, right there on a sweltering afternoon in August."

She swipes at her eyes.

"It's sad," he says. "But it was a long time ago. And we won the war. We're here. Americans. Free."

"But Zee," she says.

He hesitates. "I know something about her life," he says slowly. "I woke up last night thinking about her and those marks in the corner of the picture. The answer is right there in the drawing. I couldn't believe it."

She takes a breath. "The bundle of sticks?"

He smiles. "We have to go into Utica. You'll be able to see for yourself."

EIGHTEENTH CENTURY

That morning I thought about my life. Would it end that day? Or would I somehow have the fortune to come through the battle alive?

We kept waiting for the order to march. I heard angry mutterings; the rumbling became louder. "We'll go, with or without Herkimer!"

John leaned over, his face uncertain. "Herkimer doesn't want to leave. Some say he's afraid. Others that he fears for his men and the slaughter. He's sure that there will be an ambush. He just doesn't know where."

"What do you think?" I asked.

"He's fought before," he said. "He knows more—"

But Miller cut in. "Try not to worry about it, Zee. Remember you'll be toward the rear. You heard your father. Go back as soon as you hear—"

"Like a coward?" I said angrily.

A group of men were scrambling to move out, so there was no time for him to answer, and no choice for Herkimer. The general gave the signal to march just before they rushed headlong through the forest without him.

Miller hurried me to one of the last wagons and stood there as I climbed to the seat. He reached out. "Your father is right, Zee. You must live, even if we don't."

I shook my head.

"Don't you know we're fighting for you?" He reached up and touched my hand. He was silent for the barest second. Then he smiled. "Who could ever think you were a coward?"

He went forward and I looked after him as long as I could see his homespun jacket. "Live, Miller," I whispered, echoing my father.

At last the cart lumbered after the marching men. But after a short time, they were so far ahead that I caught only glimpses of them through the trees.

As the morning wore on, I jumped at the call of one man to another, at the metallic click of a weapon. I stared into the trees

for movement. Sitting on the rough wagon seat, I began to won-
der. The men beside me were in no hurry to move forward. They
fell farther behind, allowing wagons to overtake them and some-
how pass them on that narrow path. And then I realized. It was
deliberate. They were as afraid as I was.

Who could ever think you were a coward?

If I stayed with them, I might miss what happened in front. I
felt my lips, dry and cracked, with my rough fingers, then grasped
the side of the wagon and slid down. How easy it would be to re-
turn to Fort Dayton. Who would blame me?

Instead, I went forward. I passed one supply wagon after an-
other, feeling the strength in my legs, in my feet. I passed stragglers
ahead of the wagons. Once I stopped for water and glanced up at
the glints of the sun.

Somewhere far ahead of me were Father and John; some-
where ahead was Miller. I began to run. Branches whipped at my
hair, scratching my cheeks. I passed grim-faced men marching in
twos and threes, who barely noticed me.

I heard the terrible sound of firing; the burning smell of it
wafted back to me. The noise of muskets, of shouting, of scream-
ing, was almost deafening; the air was filled with smoke. A small
group of men retreated along the path, careening into me.

I threaded my way through them, and then through the men

who were moving forward. I ran, gasping, searching. Where was Father?

And then, without warning, men disappeared in front of me. I stopped just before I went over the edge of a deep ravine.

To go through that ravine, our men had to scramble down a log road and cross a narrow stream before they began the climb up again. The first men, led by General Herkimer, had almost reached the top when muskets began to fire and tomahawks were hurled.

My hand went to my mouth. The enemy had hidden in the dense trees on both sides of the ravine. We were surrounded.

I slid down, my hands torn by thickets, stung by nettles, my feet bleeding. At the marshy bottom men fought, blood spattered everywhere.

Herkimer had been right about the ambush. Everywhere I looked were men in British uniforms and Iroquois shrieking terrible war cries.

An old man with gray hair to his shoulders and a hatchet in his upraised hand came toward me, but then he was gone, and standing over him was one of our own, covered in blood. He yelled something to me, but it was impossible to hear.

There was no way to move back, almost no way to move forward. I stumbled over someone's legs, and confused, I thought he was sleeping, his arm bent under him, a thin line of blood staining his jacket.

He was only the first. Steps in front of me, bodies lay in awkward piles.

Someone grabbed me, holding the back of my kerchief, almost choking me.

I fought to be free of those arms, reaching back with my fingers as I was dragged into the trees, my heels digging into the ground.

The sounds I made were low and deep. I managed to turn and reached for his face, his eyes. I heard his ragged breath, and as he raised his hands against me, I twisted away.

I didn't look back; I took quick glimpses at bodies on the ground, some moving, others entirely still. Breathless, I looked at faces, at clothing, at boots and legs, searching for Father, for John. Even if their faces were covered or gone, I'd know their hands.

And Miller's hands. I remembered Miller breaking off a mushroom, and in a few quick strokes with a nail on its surface, he'd drawn Stout Lucy, the cat.

I thought then that if I saw any of them on the ground, I might not be able to keep to my own feet.

Miller.

Imagine.

What had he said that long time ago? I will draw you a hundred times, Zee, a thousand. I saw Miller tearing strips of bark from the birch tree, chunks of charcoal in his fingers, to squiggle lines and shapes. Drawing Stout Lucy, the trees, the river. Drawing me.

And I'd never given it a thought.

Above me was the sound of rumbling. A cannon? The sky darkened as if it were night, split through with jagged streaks of lightning. The rain came; huge drops spattered the blood-soaked leaves of the trees, pounded on the bodies that lay on the forest floor, puddles forming in their clothing, in the crooks of their arms or legs.

The firing died away and left only the sound of thunder rolling across the sky, and the moaning of those who were wounded. There would be no fighting, no firing, while the storm lasted. The gunpowder had to be kept dry.

As I reached the high ground on the other side of the ravine, I saw that Herkimer had been wounded. Someone propped his saddle against a beech tree, so he could direct the battle when the storm was over. He sat, pipe in his mouth, pointing, telling the men, "Stay together, two by two, back to back, one to load, one to fire."

I held my face to the rain, my mouth open; the water bathed my face, but only for a moment. A man stood alone, holding a musket. I jostled his arm. "If you show me," I said, "I can load that."

He looked at me and nodded.

The rain stopped as suddenly as it had started. The war cries began again, along with the sound of the muskets. But now Herkimer's men were in better control.

I stood against the back of that man I had never seen before, so close I could smell his fear, closer than I'd ever stood next to anyone. I tamped down the powder, working slowly with my stiff hands, working endlessly.

Then the man was on the ground, and someone pushed my head down. "Stay there. Do you want to be killed?" Not a voice I knew.

I darted away from him, not thinking about anything. Everything was color: the orange of the sun, the shiny green of the washed leaves, the red of the blood everywhere.

Father lay against a log, and I knelt next to him, my arms around him, until I was sure he was gone. I rested my head against his chest.

I saw them at home, John in the field, Mother turning the cheese pans.

And Father. Father. I held him tight.

I heard a new call. "Oonah, oonah," an Iroquois shout, repeated over and over. And someone said, "It's their call to retreat."

Was the battle over? Was this the end of it? Father dead, and so many others lying in the ravine around me, gone forever, or wounded so badly they'd never stand again.

How could John and Miller have come through this? Nothing was left. Who could tell whether we'd won or lost?

Someone pulled me to my feet. "We're going back toward Fort Dayton," the voice said. I realized it was the boy I had ridden with in the wagon the day before. "My father's gone," he said, "and the wagon."

I raised my hands helplessly. I had no energy to move.

"We can't bury the dead," he said. "The ravine has become their cemetery. Come with me."

"But my father—"

"Go along without her," a voice said.

I closed my eyes. It was Miller, alive.

Miller.

TWENTY-FIRST CENTURY

Fort Stanwix spreads itself out in front of Elizabeth and Harry. Inside the information building, open now, a plump woman wears a Revolutionary War–era dress. She loops a strand of hair back into a Zee kind of cap. "Do you have a question?"

"I know about the ravine, and the terrible ambush . . . ," Elizabeth says. Her voice trails off with embarrassment.

And now a group of kids surrounds them like a flock of chicks, waiting to ask the woman something. One even pulls at Elizabeth's sweater.

She looks at Harry helplessly. He rocks back on his feet, smiling, first at her, then at the woman, whose name tag reads *Jane*.

Harry smiling? Harry proud?

The woman leans forward. "I bet you're the smartest girl in your class."

Elizabeth steps back.

"Of course she is." Harry sounds so definite, so positive, that she feels her face flush.

They let the kids have a turn talking to the woman, and sit on a leather bench to watch a film about the battle of Oriskany.

Elizabeth thinks of what the woman said about her, of what Harry believes. That she's smart. Her throat begins to burn as she turns to Harry. "My father says I don't think," she says slowly. "I'm actually pretty useless." She raises her shoulder. "There isn't anything I do well."

Harry stops watching the film. "Tell me about Zee," he says, "or Oriskany. Or the fort. Tell me one thing."

She's silent.

"I want to hear just one fact," Harry says again.

Elizabeth searches her mind. From the fort window she sees the flag rippling in the wind.

She begins. "Colonel Gansevoort was in charge of the fort. He was not much more than a boy, and his father had told him to defend Stanwix even if it killed him. He was ready to do that, he was strong and brave, but he wanted a flag to wave over the fort, something that stood for what they were. He remembered the flag they were talking about down in Philadelphia."

Elizabeth leans toward Harry. "They ripped up the scarlet sleeve of someone's coat, the blue from someone's jacket. They cut stars from a sheet, uneven stars, but still stars, and sewed it together. It was such a makeshift thing, but when they looked up at it, they told each other they were fighting for that, a new flag, a new country . . ." Her voice trails off. "I read a little about it."

"Oh, Elizabeth," Harry says.

Her face is hot; her hands go to her cheeks.

"My mother told me," he says, "that everyone has something. Some of us are good at a lot of things, some of us are good at only one, but everyone has something."

A line of children pass, going from one room in the museum to another. She wonders about them. Which one is good in math? Good at hitting a ball? Good at singing? She has a sudden thought of Pop and his carvings, which everyone seems to admire, although she can't exactly see why.

Harry's hand is on her shoulder. "And you . . . ," he says.

She looks up at him, and he runs his finger across the tears on her cheek. "Ah, Elizabeth," he says, "you're all story."

For a moment she doesn't know what he means.

"I asked for a fact. What you gave me was so much more. Your head is filled with story." His mouth isn't steady. "How lucky you are. I'd rather have that than almost anything I can think of."

She reaches out and puts her arms around Harry. She can't even believe she's doing it.

Filled with story.

She'd rather have that than almost anything, too.

So much of what she knows about Zee has to do with story: what has been passed down to Libby and Harry, and now to her. And she has added to it. Those bits and pieces that she'll tell Pop, and maybe her own children someday.

Story.

EIGHTEENTH CENTURY

Late in the afternoon we sat together in an old woman's house, John on one side of me, Miller on the other. We filled her kitchen, the smell of battle still on our skin and clothes, coughing from the acrid smoke of muskets in our lungs.

The house was without windows, so the only light came from the hearth. I stared at the flames, wondering that anyone would have built up such a huge fire in August. I was shivering, though, and its warmth gave me comfort.

The woman passed out a cup of fermented cider, which we shared, each of us taking a mouthful. She had cut cheese from rounds and slabs of bacon, but I wasn't hungry. Would I ever be able to swallow food again?

John's face was filthy, his sparse beard matted, and his eyes closed, pale lashes clumped with tears.

Miller's head was back against the wall. He looked as if he was too tired to sleep. "They're sending General Arnold from Fort Dayton to help," he said. "He has about nine hundred troops."

"Will that be enough?" I thought about Father and the ravine and bodies piled like cords of wood on the marshy ground.

John opened his eyes. "I'll go with General Arnold. And yes, those of us who are left will be enough. This is the turning point. Look around you. We're toughened now, we can face anything. After today, we'll never give up." His eyes closed again, and he slept.

I watched the flames, sipping at the cider as the cup came around to me.

Miller stood up. "Come outside."

In the doorway I blinked at the sharp light. We walked along a path that wandered around the edge of a stream.

"I'm not going to Stanwix with General Arnold," Miller said slowly. "There's the mill at home, and a harvest waiting. I'd rather fight, but our army will need food, and I'll give everything I have to keep them going." He touched my shoulder. "Don't think I'm a coward."

I smiled at that. "Who could ever think you're a coward?" I said, echoing what he had said to me that morning. Only that morning?

"Oriskany will not be the end of the war," Miller said. "It's still the beginning. It will be years, Zee, but John is right. We are going to win."

I thought about going home, but there was no home.

"Come with me, Zee."

I turned to look up at him. I saw him building the henhouse, nails in his mouth. I saw him swinging me in the snow, laughing. How had I not seen what he was like? Who he truly was?

"Someday," he said, "I'll draw you standing outside the house we'll build."

I held out my scarred hands.

"Ah, your hands," he said, and then I could see he was trying to smile. "Perhaps you'll ruin the soap, and burn the bread. You may leave the gates open so the animals will wander free, and I'll draw all of that. But I'll draw you with strength in your face, because no one has more."

I thought of the drawing of Stout Lucy and the day I'd seen him work on it.

"If I had something, I'd draw you now," he said.

I reached under the handkerchief at my neck. The map was

still there, and I gave it to him to use the other side. "But I have no cap," I said.

He smiled. "Do you think I can't remember?"

I sat there watching.

I had to go on to Fort Stanwix. I had to do my own part in this fight for our freedom. I wouldn't tell him that yet, though, not until he finished the drawing.

TWENTY-FIRST CENTURY

Harry pulls his dusty truck up to an equally dusty storefront in Utica. "This place has been here for as long as I can remember."

Elizabeth glances at the window. There are stacks of chipped plates, an ancient jade plant in the center, and a pair of lamps with rosettes twirling around their bases.

"Everything stays the same," Harry says. "I don't think they've sold anything in twenty years. How they stay in business is a mystery. I stop in sometimes and wander around."

Inside, there's a musty smell; motes of dust dance across the back window.

Harry nods at the owner and takes Elizabeth's elbow; they wend their way around old furniture to the side wall, where paintings in curlicue frames hang in uneven lines. "Not these," Harry says, "it's the drawings I want you to see."

He's excited. Elizabeth's heart picks up. What has he found?

They walk past paintings of stiff women and bearded men, and in the very back are the drawings. "Do you remember"—Harry smiles down at her—"the mark on Zee's drawing?"

"A bundle of sticks, tied in the middle." She looks at the drawing in front of her. It has the same marks. "The same artist," she breathes.

The owner comes up in back of them. He looks as old as the store itself, with gray hair to his shoulders, tiny glasses. "That's a sheaf of wheat," he says. "It was his mark. I don't think he could read. Miller Wheeler was his name." He waves his hand toward the wall. "I have two of his drawings. There are others in a museum in Albany."

Elizabeth looks up at them. The first is a field, and two boys are fighting, rolling on the ground, drawn with just a few lines, but she can feel the movement, the energy of it. Looking on is a girl. And in back of them is a river. The Delaware River, of course. Is it Zee? Only her profile is visible. "Are they her children?"

"I don't think so." The owner shrugs. "She looks younger than the boys who are fighting, doesn't she?"

Elizabeth leans forward. "It might have been before the war," she says, "before Zee went to Oriskany. A warm day, maybe, and they've been planting. They stop—"

"You like to tell stories," the owner says, and she feels that burst of happiness in her chest.

"It's the next one you'll want to see," Harry says gently.

Elizabeth takes a step; her hand goes out. It's Zee,

Elizabeth would know her anywhere: that button nose, those apple cheeks. But it's an older Zee, a laughing Zee. She stands at the edge of the same field, holding a toddler, and two boys stand next to her. If it weren't for the old-fashioned clothes, they could be standing there today.

"After Oriskany," Elizabeth begins slowly, "a Loyalist named Han Yost Schuyler told St. Leger that the Patriot side's General Arnold was coming. He pointed to the trees, as if to say, 'with as many men as there are leaves.' "

Harry finishes for her. "St. Leger retreated, leaving Fort Stanwix to the Americans."

Was Zee there? Did she see the flag flying over the fort? They'll never know that. But Elizabeth is sure the war was over when Miller Wheeler drew Zee and the children. Their children, she's sure of it.

"Yes," Harry says, even though Elizabeth hasn't said it aloud, and he buys the drawings, of course.

"Zee for you," he says. "And the field . . ."

Elizabeth expects him to say "for me."

Instead, he says, "The field for Libby."

On the way back to Libby's house, Elizabeth clutches the drawings to her. In his way, Miller has told her the story. She can picture Zee as an old lady with white hair under her cap and dozens of grandchildren, one of them Elizabeth's own great-great-great-grandmother.

PATRICIA REILLY GIFF is the author of many beloved books for children, including the Zigzag Kids series, the Kids of the Polk Street School books, the Friends and Amigos books, and the Polka Dot Private Eye books. Several of her novels for older readers have been chosen as ALA-ALSC Notable Children's Books and ALA-YALSA Best Books for Young Adults. They include *The Gift of the Pirate Queen; All the Way Home; Nory Ryan's Song*, a Society of Children's Book Writers and Illustrators Golden Kite Honor Book for Fiction; and the Newbery Honor Books *Lily's Crossing* and *Pictures of Hollis Woods*. *Lily's Crossing* was also chosen as a *Boston Globe–Horn Book* Honor Book. Her most recent books include *Water Street, Eleven*, and *Wild Girl*. Patricia Reilly Giff lives in Connecticut.

EIGHTEENTH CENTURY

On a beautiful spring morning, I stood at the edge of the field with Rachael in my arms and the boys, tall now, next to me.

The war was over. How long ago it seemed.

After the British left Fort Stanwix without a fight, John and I came home together. On the way, we stopped, trying to find Mother's small things, but my cave was gone, buried somewhere under stone or mud from a storm.

But that wasn't the important thing. It was the land that meant everything, our land for which we had fought so hard.

At last, we reached our own green field. Miller found us there; he came toward us, arms out.

I told Toby and Matthew the story of the war; soon Rachael

will be old enough to hear it, too. I'll tell her about the dear ones we lost. I'll promise her we'll always be free.

Because it was spring, I reminded the boys of Old Gerard and what he had told me years before. "Look up. See the oak leaves like furry mouse ears? That means it's time to plant." The boys laughed as I added my own words: "Whisper to the seeds. Tell them to be happy down there."

I knew they'd remember those words when they helped their father with the planting, then helped John and his boys, and Julian across the river.

Miller glanced up from the drawing he was doing of the four of us. "Ah, Zee," he said. "So many stories to tell."

I nodded, smiling through a quick glint of tears as I remembered. Hard stories, some of them.

But now I smelled the bread baking. I had to hurry before it burned again.

TWENTY-FIRST CENTURY

It's Tuesday night. Elizabeth has spent her last day in school exchanging hugs and e-mail addresses.

Now the duffel bags are in the hall. Elizabeth and Libby stand next to the door, waiting. Pop has called on his cell phone to say that he's just pulled off the highway. He'll be there any minute.

Elizabeth looks up at Zee in her thin silver frame, and next to Elizabeth, Libby has tears in her eyes. "You're coming back," she says fiercely. "You're your father's girl, but you belong to us, too, now."

Harry has said almost the same thing. "In July," he says, "we'll search around together and see if we can find the old caves. Three cousins, why not?"

They probably won't find anything, but it doesn't make any difference. She'll come back for a long visit.

Zee has changed her life.

But as she sees Pop's car pull up, she can't wait. She opens the door and runs outside. He's given her all this; for the first time she realizes it. What had he said? It's time for you to know your mother's family.

She stops in the middle of the path as he opens the door. She's going home to find out about Pop, about his carvings, and about what it's like to have a daughter who spills things, who's a little bit messy, but who loves him. She's going to find out his story. And she's going to make sure he knows hers.

She can't wait to begin.

author's note

Fort Stanwix was built by the British but fell into disuse before the Revolutionary War. The Patriots rebuilt it, renaming it Fort Schuyler. After Colonel St. Leger's failed attempts to capture it in 1777, the fort was damaged by fire and heavy rain; it was abandoned in 1781. The fort, once again called Stanwix, has been restored for visitors. Throughout this book I have called it Fort Stanwix, as it was known originally and is still called today.

After he was wounded, Colonel Nicholas Herkimer was taken back to his house in what is now Little Falls, New York. He died of infection several days later. The house is a museum now, and is open to the public.

ACKNOWLEDGMENTS

I'm truly grateful to everyone at the Schenectady County Public Library for their help, and especially to Mary Trivilino for her warmth and encouragement; to Robert Sullivan for his patience, expert knowledge, and willingness to answer my questions, which made all the difference; and to Karen Bradley, who made sure I had a place to work and everything I needed. A wonderful library; wonderful librarians.

I wish to thank Wendy Lamb, my editor, and George Nicholson for their support, and of course, my family: my husband, Jim; my children, Jim, Bill, and Alice. I'm blessed by their love.

SEP   2010